To Shirley with best wishes, Always, Dave Nickel
CHRISTMAS 2020

The Broom
by Drew Nickell

© Copyright 1995; 2020 Drew Nickell

ISBM 978-1-953278-13-5 Hard Back
ISBN 978-1-953278-11-1 Soft Back
ISBN 978-1-953278-12-8 E-Book

All rights reserved. No part of this publication may be reproduced, stored in a retrieval system, or transmitted in any form or by any means – electronic, mechanical, photocopy, recording, or any other – except for brief quotations in printed reviews, without the prior written permission of the author.

This is a work of fiction. The characters are both actual and fictitious. With the exception of verified historical events and persons, all incidents, descriptions, dialogue and opinions expressed are the products of the author's imagination and are not to be construed as real.

Published by

Indignor House, Inc.
Chesapeake, VA 23322

www.IndignorHouse.com

The Broom

Drew Nickell

For Amanda, and her children …

Introduction

High above a ridge in Virginia's Blue Ridge Mountains lived an old woman about whom no one seemed to know very much. She lived in a rickety old house that was delicately situated on a slope near the top of an ancient mountain, which came to be known as Devil's Knob. Far below her one window, a hamlet of five or six homes sat as though they were miniatures. Since the old woman's eyes had long since become weakened from age, she could hardly see much of what was happening. She spent most of her time sitting in a rocking chair with her back to the window and her feet propped upon a stool. Always, she enjoyed sitting in front of her warm fireplace. From time to time, she walked outside onto her porch where one end rested on a bent post driven deeply into the steep incline of a hill. She would gather several pieces of weathered firewood before returning to her tiny house. The fire never died because she only maintained a small fire enough to sustain a constant low burn.

Although she retained little in the way of personal belongings, she kept in the corner toward the rear of the house an ancient broom. It was made from a style of the middle 1600's and its gnarled handle attested to its authenticity. Above all else, the old woman treasured this broom.

Every once in a while, she glanced over at it and laughed before looking back on a long-ago memory, recalling the events and how all of this came to pass.

Chapter 1

By the middle of the 1700's, the western migration was edging its way nearer to the Ohio River. An exploratory jaunt led by Governor William Spotswood and his fabled Knights of the Golden Horseshoe had earlier revealed an unfettered land, rich in milk and honey, that they named the Shenandoah Valley. The following decades saw wave after wave of Scotch-Irish and German immigrants descend upon the valley who tilled the nutrient-rich soil and thus established a vast granary. That was just the beginning when the Rockfish River area was settled to the west of where Jefferson erected Monticello.

Nathan Green occupied a modest house along the river, which spilled down the southeastern slope of Afton Mountain. He dug a toiled existence in the rich but rocky soil. His farm would eventually become known as Greenfield. To the northwest was Afton Mountain and toward the southwest a bit further away, Devil's Knob rose to meet the setting sun. Evenings came early on Greenfield Farm, especially in autumn. The fiercely chilled winds began in mid-October and ushered in a harbinger of the colder season. As the reds and yellows fell from spindly limbs and lit the ground as if a fading fire, Nathan busily gathered pumpkins from the fields that had already produced a modest crop of corn. The night was approaching, and he wanted to stoke his fireplace.

As the sun dipped below the crest of Devil's Knob, Nathan placed the last of the pumpkins into a pile near the barn. It was dark when he finally put the last of his implements away. As the howling wolves greeted the rise of an amber moon, Nathan rushed into the house with an armful of firewood. The howling grew louder. He shivered. Stoking the glowing coals, the fire slowly warmed his modest home. Nathan suspended an iron pot from a hook and the sweet aroma emanated from the bubbling stew.

He savored the last spoonful of his supper when the howling suddenly stopped. A knock at his oaken door startled him. Nathan stared at the door trying to remember where he placed his musket. A second knock made him jump and he dropped the bowl and spoon onto the floor.

With the third knock, he stuttered. "Who is it?"

"Open the door Nathan." It was a low but distinctly female voice.

Nathan walked toward the door. Opening it he found a small, yet aged woman, and he motioned her in. She looked up at him and laughed.

"You don't know who I am do you?"

"No ma 'am," he said, his mouth ajar.

"Well, I brought you *from your mother* and I *named* you."

Nathan's eyes widened. His mother had died giving him life. It was his father who raised him. Six years before, Nathan's father joined Nathan's mother never once talking about his wife. Nathan was twelve when his father briefly told him the difficulty with which he was brought into this world. He never mentioned who else was on hand to witness the birth of a baby and the death of his mother.

It was something of a family secret that was kept from him until now. The older woman standing before him was about to tell him a story, and Nathan was listening intently.

Chapter 2

Nathan's mother, Sarah, was born to a prosperous family of planters. They earned their fortune from tobacco that they grew on a large Tidewater plantation. Home schooled in the finer arts of cooking, dancing and sewing, his mother was beautiful yet frail. She was sixteen when she married Isaac Green. Isaac had been apprenticed to a carpenter in Williamsburg but found life in crowded Williamsburg not to his liking. On business and while visiting the plantation that was Sarah's home, Isaac met the beautiful but thin Sarah, and the two fell instantly in love.

As the days passed into months, Isaac found excuses to call on Sarah's father just to lay his eyes upon Sarah. One spring morning, Isaac rode to the plantation to ask for her hand in marriage. He spoke plainly to Sarah's father telling him of his disenchantment with city life and of his plans to settle a hundred miles to the west. With reservations, Sarah's father agreed to the marriage, and two weeks hence, the couple was joined together in the stately brick home that overlooked the James River. Following the wedding and lavishly endowed reception, the young couple set off for the western hills. Given the slimness of chance she would again see her family, Sarah tearfully bade her father farewell and set off with her wide-eyed husband.

The journey of two weeks was especially difficult for the Greens, as the roads to the west of the fledgling capital of Richmond were not well kept. At long last, they arrived at the foot of the Blue Ridge. After staking out a claim to a hundred acres, of which no experienced planter would dare trifle, Isaac set about building a modest house from the local hardwood. Sarah utilized her scant knowledge of planting to sow a vegetable garden of green beans, butter beans, corn and squash. The work was painfully slow. As trees felled and the house formed, the frail but determined wife scratched at the hard soil between the stumps in order that they might eat. As the first frost appeared and the house was complete, they survived the first winter on the fruits of Sarah's labor. Even though the daughter of a wealthy planter might typically have been spoiled from the work of others, Sarah attacked her new life with not a hint of disdain but with all her energy. She set upon helping to establish a home for herself and her husband. As the snow thawed and the Rockfish River surged with runoff, Isaac caught trout that nourished his wife who was now swelling around her abdomen. He lovingly shooed her back into the house when she repeatedly attempted to help him turn the cold, moist soil that surrounded their home. Instead, she set about sewing their clothes with the bolts of cloth she had received as wedding presents.

Occasionally, she reached for her leather-bound Bible that was given to her by the minister of Bruton Parish Church, who had married the couple the year before. Her eyes tiring, she returned the book to the shelf and prepared their supper. Sometimes, Isaac returned with an opossum or a few squirrels or, when luck was with him, a buck that augmented their diet for several days with fresh meat. Life passed slowly that spring, with the days lengthened and the steady northern approach of the sun's path across the Virginia sky.

As spring turned to summer, Sarah's swelling abdomen slowed her gait and the small life that dwelled within grew restless. Isaac knew his wife would soon bear their child. He inquired about a midwife at the adjacent farms. He learned of one who lived alone on the side of the mountain overlooking his farm. This surprised him because he knew of no one who lived at such a high elevation. Regardless, Isaac was determined to secure the woman's services so as to aid his frail wife in the birth of their child.

Chapter 3

The climb up Devil's Knob was difficult and took several painstaking hours. What scant trail there was, was poorly marked and overgrown. The air felt to be much cooler with each step. Isaac carried his musket in the event it would be needed. However, he soon discovered it worked better as a walking stick of sorts. As he neared the crest of the Blue Ridge, he saw the small house that was set into the slope of the mountain's side. It was well past midday when Isaac stepped onto the woman's porch and knocked at her door.

With the third knock, the door opened from the force of Isaac's knuckles and revealed a single room. A table with one chair and a rocking chair and a small stool were the only furnishings. A low fire glowed in the fireplace, and it belied the otherwise abandoned appearance of the small house. The only attempt at decoration was an oval braided rug situated between the table and the hearth. In the far left-hand corner stood a broom typical of the time, and yet, its handle seemed to be worn and nicked.

Isaac called out, "Anyone here?"

No answer. He waited for what seemed like an eternity. The door, which he had left opened, slammed shut. Startled, Isaac stood alone in the single room. He breathed deeply and resigned himself to the possibility that the wind blew the door shut. Feeling a need to return home, he pulled the door open and stepped onto the porch. Looking in all directions, he realized he was alone. One more attempt to call out to anyone within earshot produced no result, so he slowly began his descent home.

By the time the downward slope flattened out at the edge of his farm, it was nearly dark. He called to his wife. He always called out to her after returning from a hunting expedition so as not to frighten her. The window was illuminated from the fire within, and he enjoyed the sweet aroma of freshly baked cornbread. He stepped onto his porch and embraced his wife.

"Nothing?" Sarah inquired noticing only the musket in his arms. She did not know of the actual reason for today's hike. He felt it better for her not to know.

"Uh … no dearest," he replied. "No such fortune today."

"Well, we still have some of yesterday's stew for your supper and …"

"I smelled the cornbread from over yonder." He smiled.

Sarah laughed and the two went inside. Sitting at the table and bowing their heads, Isaac thanked God for the meal and for looking after his wife during today's absence. Often, he did just that upon returning after having left to hunt for wild game. A silent serenity filled the room, and all seemed right with the world.

They finished the last of the stew when Isaac inquired about his unborn child. He did this with frequency, of late, and Sarah beamed at his interest.

"I think we're getting mighty close," she said. "Your son was kicking an awful lot today." She always referred to their unborn baby in the masculine sense.

"Who says it going to be a son?" Isaac teased.

"I have no doubt as to that being the case," she retorted smiling.

"If you're so sure, what are we going to name this 'son'?"

"That's yours to say, you're the father."

"I hope you're going to be all right," Isaac said frowning with the concern about his wife's frail demeanor.

"I'll be all right," she reassured him patting his hand. "I'll be all right."

Isaac remained doubtful but took great care in not showing this. The conversation ended as the dishes were cleared from the table.

If only I could have found that old woman today, Isaac thought to himself, *if only she could come here and help my Sarah.*

He decided that he would make another attempt in two or three days. He blew out the candles, kissed his wife and said, "Good night dearest."

"Good night Isaac," she mumbled drifting off to sleep.

Chapter 4

As the sun's early rays shone crimson in the eastern sky, Isaac arose being careful not to wake his wife. She tossed and turned throughout the night and he wanted her to get as much rest as possible. He poked at the coals of the waning fire and added a few pieces of wood. He watched as the flames darted toward the dark chimney. He poked at the fire some more and added two larger logs. He waited until the flames convinced him of their chances and ate some of the cornbread from their previous meal.

He stepped onto the porch and glanced toward the river. The air was already laden with the humidity that stifles the body during summer's peak. Isaac whispered that it needed to rain. He stopped for a moment, wondering when Sarah would begin her labor and silently prayed for an easy delivery. As he stood there, thinking about his wife and all they accomplished in less than two years, he watched and listened as the river rolled over the large rocks. It astounded him that the river, as with the mountains behind, paid him no mind and yet they had become such a part of his world. He pondered this mystery when Sarah stirred about inside their cabin.

"Have you been up long?" she asked not looking in his direction. She placed a dish on the table.

"Not long. I ate some of the cornbread and I want you to eat the rest."

"I don't need —"

"Sarah you need to eat, remember you're —"

"I know ... eating for two," she replied in a mocking voice, which was followed by a gentle laugh. She sat with some difficulty as the life that dwelled within her was now bulging from her abdomen. Not as obvious to her husband was the reality that the baby was also sapping her strength with its steady growth.

"I should move along and see if I can get some work done," said Isaac. "Are you going to be all right?"

"I'll be fine." Looking up at him, she smiled and added, "See if you can catch some fish today. I've got a hankering for some of that trout you've been pulling out of that river lately."

Isaac stepped off of the porch and headed for the water's edge. He set three lines baited with worms he had dug from the fields. His own father liked to fish and had taught his son well. But all that training, as well as the worms, would produce nothing on that day.

Perhaps the fish themselves are too hot to eat, Isaac thought. After a few hours of fishing to no avail, he stated aloud, "They ain't biting, they just ain't biting at all."

He walked to the fields and, as Sarah had taught him to do, picked at the ground between the rows of corn and yanked out the stubborn weeds. He noticed that the corn was showing some tassel as he thought to himself that this would be a fine crop. *Sarah's taken a city-born carpenter's apprentice and turned him into quite a field hand,* he thought as he poked at the ground.

When the sun was high, a faint rumbling of thunder threatened from the distance. Isaac already removed his shirt, and his trousers were soaked with perspiration. A soft breeze stirred the young, tasseled cornstalks, and Isaac leaned backwards and relished in the cooling wind. He turned to the southwest and saw the blackened sky.

I'd best be going inside now, he thought. *We're in for quite a storm.*

Living alongside the Blue Ridge taught one to be prepared for drastic sudden changes in weather. Storms would arise in summer when warm, moist air from the tropics collided head-on with the cool, dry air from Canada. The ensuing violent struggle of diametrically opposed air masses most frequently caromed off either side of the Blue Ridge creating havoc for life below. In his time, neither Isaac Green nor any of his contemporaries enjoyed meteorological knowledge, but those who dwelled in the area of Virginia's Blue Ridge learned that the weather could nevertheless change at a moment's notice.

Isaac, soaked in perspiration as he was, gathered his hat, shirt and hoe and ran toward the lean-to at the rear of his house. The rain fell by the time he arrived. Circling around to the side, he put a lead around his goat and struggled to coax it beneath the protective covering. He tied a boson's knot to the supporting post of the lean-to and then circled around toward the steps. By the time he arrived at the porch, the wind and rain raged all around him. Water poured in horizontal sheets as though it was tossed from buckets. Trees teetered to-and-fro, as if a handkerchief waved by a hand. A flash, followed by a crack, caused Isaac to jump. Taking a step backwards, he watched in amazement at the scene unfolding before his very eyes and was appalled at how quickly this storm had come upon him. The rows of corn tossed back and forth as though they had neither roots nor stalks of their own. More lightning, more thunder, more wind and rain. Still winded from his run up to the house and with amazement in nature's anger, Isaac Green squinted to see if the river had picked up speed. A brief respite in the horizontal waves of rain allowed but only a glimpse. Surely enough, the Rockfish River was rolling faster, swelled by the additional water.

I just hope the corn survives all of this wind, Isaac said to himself. *My, my it's coming down now ...*

"ISAAC!" the voice from his wife was uncharacteristically harsh and well hewn at the edges.

Isaac entered to find his wife sprawled across the bed and covered in sweat. Her hair tossed as if it hadn't been brushed; she looked to be in agony.

"Sarah?" He rushed towards her and grabbed her. "What in the world …?"

"It's time, Isaac, it's time," she whimpered letting out a gasp of air with her words.

"My God the baby," Isaac whispered, barely within earshot of his wife. "The baby's coming. Oh Sarah."

Chapter 5

Nathan hardly spoke another word that evening. The old woman told him everything about the night in which he was born. She spoke in a low, grating monotone and stopped only long enough to cough. Each time she coughed, she followed by clearing her throat. It reminded Nathan of a buck saw grinding on a hard knot in the grain of an otherwise soft pine tree. Not only did he remain silent, but he hardly blinked. She told him about the difficulty that women — particularly frail women — had when giving birth for the first time. She told him how she arrived during a fierce storm with only a broom in her hand. It was the very same broom she was holding now. She pointed to teeth marks in the broom's handle and as there seemed to be several, she indicated the ones that belonged to his own mother. He frowned and stared at the old woman seemingly confused as to why his mother, or any woman for that matter, would sink her teeth into the handle of a broom. Yet he remained silent.

"It's to kill the pain boy," she said harshly. It was as if she knew exactly what he was thinking. She then laughed briefly, coughed and continued. She explained that his mother died within minutes of giving birth. His father, distraught, told her that as far as he was concerned, she might as well name the boy herself.

"That's how you got your name, Nathan." She almost smiled at him. The two stared at each other for a moment not speaking. In the distance, the long low howl of a lone wolf broke the silence. The old woman looked up over her shoulder with a sudden jerk of her head. "My time grows nigh." She drew out the last syllable in a distracted manner.

"So, where'd you get the name Nathan from?"

She squinted and replied, "That's another story for another day boy."

A gust of wind blew the shutters open and knocked the candle off of the sill extinguishing its flame. He stood and fumbled around for it in the dim glow of light cast from the fireplace. Finding it, he closed the shutter, secured it and re-lit the candle. With that, he turned around to find that he was alone. Returning to his chair, he stared at the fire thinking about what he had just learned and meshed this with the scant information he had learned from his father.

The wind's howling returned, along with the distant howling of wolves. He shivered again, rose from his seat and neared closer to the fire. Picking up a log, he set it on the coals. Outside, the wind and the wolves howled long into the eternal night as Nathan Green sat staring at the fire listening.

Chapter 6

On the morning following the birth of her firstborn, Sarah Tucker Green was buried beneath the elm tree that stood between the home she had helped to build and the river that had once quenched her thirst. Isaac wept as he raised his pick and thrust it into the hard soil. It was slow labor to dig what he never imagined he would have to dig. His crying added to the difficulty of unearthing such a grave. Climbing out of the hole, he looked into the sky and noticed that the sun was almost directly overhead. As he lowered Sarah into the grave, wrapped in the sheet that had covered their bed, he sobbed pitifully as there was no one present with whom he might have shared his grief. Somehow, he had the foresight to bring along the Bible that had been given to his wife by the man who joined them together in Williamsburg. He tried to read aloud the Twenty-third Psalm, but it was hopeless. As he read in silence, the tears streamed down his cheeks and dripped onto the pages. The only words that came to his lips were, "I'll give this to your son Sarah."

Even though returning the earth to the hole was far less laborious, it seemed more difficult to Isaac, nevertheless. He turned away and walked back to the house. It had not occurred to him how strange it was that the old midwife had managed to show in time to deliver the baby. Yet upon entering the house, he was surprised to find the baby lying on the floor wrapped in a blanket and crying.

On the table was a note with the words *give Nathan goat milk*, and it wasn't long before Isaac realized that this was a directive from the old woman. He stepped outside to milk the goat and then returned to the crying baby. After pouring the milk into a small cup, he carefully dribbled the milk into his son's mouth. He knew then he had to raise the boy without the help of a mother. As the newborn vigorously swallowed the nourishing milk, Isaac vowed that he would do his very best in caring for the one thing that remained from his beloved wife. He owed it to her memory to raise the boy as best as he could. Although he would try to give every ounce of love in his heart to Nathan, he never recovered from the utter sense of loneliness that overcame him that morning.

The experience of the birth of their child coinciding with the death of his wife left Isaac deeply scarred. The years rolled by as did the river outside. Summer begot autumn. Autumn begot winter. Winter begot spring and spring was the procreator of summer, over and over with ever increasing velocity. Still, the passing of the years never dulled the sharpness of the pain he felt in his heart.

Chapter 7

By the time Nathan was eight years old, rumors of a revolt against the Crown of England had spread to the Rockfish River area. Isaac had little interest in politics, nor for that matter anything else beyond the confines of his farm. When Nathan, who had begun his schooling the year before, was asked if he was going to fight George III replied, *'that's someone else's fight, not mine.'* That was that.

Nathan, despite his youth, learned early not to press his father for details beyond the scant information he *was* given. He knew little about his mother — only that she died the night he was born and that she left him her Bible. His father only briefly answered any questions put to him about his mother before quickly changing the subject. For that matter, life on a Virginia farm in the late 1770's was neither short on activity nor long on unoccupied hours. There were plenty of chores, and Nathan learned much from his father about the rudiments of farming, fishing, hunting and, above all else, survival.

Isaac took great care in seeing to it that Nathan was educated in ciphering and reading and writing. He realized, early on, that he was ill equipped to do so himself, so he arranged to send the boy to a tutor at a local farm about five miles down-river. Each morning, six days a week,

Isaac mounted the mule and rode with the boy to the one room schoolhouse only to return in the afternoon.

Nathan, now in his second year of school, was riding the mule alone to and from school. He incurred his father's wrath only one time when it became obvious that he lied about attending school and had gone fishing instead. Even then, after being punished with a switch from a weeping willow tree, Isaac told his son never to lie to him again. From the pain that Nathan saw in his father's eyes, there was no way he could ever *think* of hurting the man again.

As the years passed, Nathan and his father grew close. It was a silent understanding that they had for each other, rather than a more direct and vocal relationship built on conversation. His father marveled at the way the boy grew into young manhood. It was helpful to him that his son had become a very good shot, for instance, for his own eyesight had faded with the years. He enjoyed fishing for it demanded neither sharpness of the eyes nor steadiness of the hands, and it was relaxing to cool his feet in the rapids of the Rockfish River. Yet, for the rest of his life, there was always a quiet melancholy about him, something he could not shake, and it was this sadness that always entered Nathan's mind whenever he pondered the silence of his father.

On his twelfth birthday, Isaac told the boy briefly about the difficulty his mother had giving birth. But he did not elaborate to any real degree. He never mentioned that there was anyone else present. When Nathan heard rumors of an old witch living in the mountains, he asked his father about it. His father shrugged and denied any knowledge of the old woman. It wasn't as if he had misled him. After that terrible night, his father just never saw the old woman again.

After all, his father owed her a debt of gratitude for being there when she was sorely needed and disclosing where the woman lived would hardly seem the proper thing to do. Isaac said often that he didn't need to look for trouble. Enough came looking for him on its own. More importantly, he lived his quiet life by this credo and, as with his refusal to fight for independence from England, this served him well. After all,

Nathan already lost his mother, therefore what good could come from losing his father? As far as independence was concerned, Isaac Green had plenty of it with much to spare by living his life and scratching out a meek living in the rocky soil along the banks of the Rockfish River. It mattered little to him what country he lived in.

It was about the time of Nathan's sixteenth year when news of the 1782 surrender of Lord Cornwallis reached the remote farms of Nelson County. Nathan was caught up in the fervor that newly won independence had created among the county's youth. He tried to excite his father about it, hoping to create something the two could enjoy talking about. It was of no use. Politics held no sway for Isaac Green. Lately, he seemed to grow more distant and quieter with the passage of each year.

One spring day in the year of 1784, Isaac sent Nathan into nearby Schuyler for some supplies. The ride would take the better part of a day and Nathan enjoyed the diversions that such a trip was sure to provide. Upon his return, Nathan found his father lying beneath the elm tree atop his mother's grave. He tried to wake him but to no avail. Eighteen years after she had passed, Sarah Tucker Green was joined by the husband who loved her. He cried softly at the loss of his father, but with his tears, Nathan knew that his father was now with the woman he missed. At long last, they were together forever.

Under an ancient elm tree, located along the banks of the Rockfish River, stood two simple markers with the names of Sarah and Isaac Green. Beneath their names were etched the years 1766 and 1784, respectively, preceded only by the solitary letter — D.

Chapter 8

Nathan Green buried his father alongside his mother six and one-half years before he was visited by the old woman who told him about the night he was born. He finished his formal education when he was sixteen and spent the ensuing eight years farming the land of his father.

Since his father's death, he experimented with pumpkins and other forms of squash. Once a month, he traveled to Charlottesville spending time with the Virginia Militia. He regretted that he was not among Washington's soldiers during the war but nevertheless marched proudly. He particularly enjoyed hearing stories told by many of the veterans.

The United States were in their infancy; soon they would proclaim the heroic Washington as their first president. Thomas Jefferson, who was building a large mansion at nearby Monticello, was among the prominent Virginia delegates to the Congress that was busy hammering out something called a Constitution. With him were James Madison of Montpelier and young James Monroe of nearby Ash Lawn-Highland all of whom enjoyed great reputations in Virginia.

Unaware that history was being written during the times that he lived, Nathan busied himself with monthly maneuvers in the Militia spending the rest of his hours tending to his fields. He read everything he could get his hands on, which wasn't a lot to speak of. He read his mother's

Bible by candlelight in the evenings before his eyes grew weary and he'd drift off to sleep. What he learned from his father and personal experience ensured that he would never know of hunger although, at times, his plate was lean.

He grew to be a strapping young man, broad of chest and heavy of beard. His attempts to converse with the young ladies at nearby farms often ended in stammering disasters that brought on a chorus of giggles. Yet, his good looks and knowledge that he was *landed* never escaped the females he encountered.

He took a particular interest in a young lady who lived at the farm where he had schooled. Her name was Anne Wood, and her father operated a gristmill on the south end of a farm — a farm started a few years before Isaac and Sarah Green were married. Anne's father was a lieutenant in General Washington's army and took some umbrage at the fact that Nathan's father was unwilling to join in the cause of independence. Since Isaac had taken great care to promptly cover his share of the teacher's stipend and knowing that Nathan took an active part in the postwar militia, Lieutenant Wood tolerated Nathan's attentions toward his daughter. Yet, he was careful not to encourage a courtship. Her father was hoping she would find another who, perhaps, would come from a family with some prestige or wealth or preferably, both.

At first, Anne did not really know what to think of her would-be suitor. For the last two years he seemed to happen by with greater frequency, all the while stuttering through the most ridiculous excuses as to what brought him down to Wood's Mill. He was handsome enough, to be sure, and his own apparent strength made him seem to be quite a catch for any young lady. It wasn't that he was stupid, or anything of the like, but his overall demeanor and methods of speech seemed *awkward*. Her mother coached her to be nonchalant and disengaging when approached by young men, and her seeming indifference did little to encourage Nathan's poor attempts to attract her favorable attentions.

Nathan was *awed* by Anne Wood. Her graceful form, satin-smooth skin, elegant features and voluptuous bosom sent him into a stammering fit, even if not for her apparent indifference. Lately, he had trouble sleeping because he could not remove her vision from his own mind. Sometimes, he tried to rid his thoughts of her by staying away from her father's farm. Nevertheless, he arrived upon some poor excuse to journey down-river and frittered away the hours until she stepped onto the front steps of her father's stately home.

She would come out on those occasions, raise her chin in the most provocative way, lift her arched eyebrows and inquire as to what had brought him to Wood's Mill. Stumbling through an excuse that was ill-fated from its inception, he tried offering it up anyway. Deep inside, she was happy that he came by but was careful not to let on. Often, she peeked at him through the curtains of an upstairs window giggling at the way he nervously paced around the front yard. It was as though he couldn't remember what he was looking for. She knew exactly what, or whom, he was seeking and she enjoyed putting Nathan through the agony of awaiting her arrival on the stairs. She never admitted it to anyone, but she was as attracted to him as he was to her. Still, she continued to play this masquerade of indifference with all of the savvy her mother instilled in her. She was quite good at it.

One day while peeking at Nathan through the curtains, her father asked what she was doing. Attempting to dodge the question, she arrived at an excuse as lame as anything Nathan could have conjured. She was stunned to discover that her father already invited the young man to dinner. She ran to her room, opened the wardrobe and spent the next twenty minutes searching for just the right dress to wear.

Little did Nathan know what he was in for. Surely after dinner he would have to find just the right words to say to Lieutenant Wood as he intended to ask him for his daughter's hand. However, he would have to get through dinner first and take great care not to knock over the glass of claret before him. It was to be the longest meal in his young life, and throughout the years to follow, he never forgot that wonderful afternoon he spent dining with the Woods.

Chapter 9

Not quite a century had passed since the notorious Salem Witch Trials of 1692 when Nathan Green was invited to dine with the family of Lieutenant Josiah Wood. The colonies of the 1690's had, in the course of nine decades, become the United States of America. Contemporaries of the 1780's were hardly impressed with the threat of witchcraft that absolutely crippled the Massachusetts Bay Colony in the previous century. Rumors of a mountaintop witch thus became a great source of entertainment and gossip to the Nelson County residents.

In 1689, with Puritan rule fading, Cotton Mather published *Memorable Providences Relating to Witchcraft and Possessions*. The sensational work gripped its readers with the fear of an impending pandemic of witchcraft and, in particular, affected young readers who were impressionable with that which was strange and unknown. One of these youths, a shy and retiring girl of fifteen, had read Mather's book and told her friends about symptoms indicative of being a witch. Among these girls, an eleven-year-old named Abigail Adams asked her uncle's slave, Tituba, about what she had heard. Tituba, who spent her early years in the West Indies, recounted the legends of voodoo and stories of zombies and witchcraft associated with her own youth. Abigail brought along her cousin, Betty Parris, and with their friends became enchanted with the stories being told by Tituba. Inevitably, the resulting nightmares gave way to fits of screaming and witchcraft hysteria that took hold of Salem much in the same way that fire takes hold of dried hay stacked in a barn.

Before that fire was extinguished, one hundred-fifty poor suspects stood trial; fourteen women and five men hung from the gallows and one old man was even pressed to death with boulders stacked on his chest. Countless others, in fear for their own lives, fled Salem for points to the south and west. In the wake of such hysteria, many were glad to be rid of Salem even if it meant leaving their friends, neighbors, loved ones and homes far behind. In some cases, the ones who stayed to defend themselves lived only to meet the lash or the noose, in the end. A whisper here, or an ill-timed sneeze there, was often enough to bring on accusations, indictments and trials.

It was all just beginning when Lydia Thorn, an indentured servant living in the house adjacent to the Parris' house, fell in love with Nathan Parris, Betty's older brother. Lydia was all of sixteen and serving the final two years of her seven-year indentureship to the Adams family who had paid for her passage from London. With her flaxen hair and sapphire eyes, Lydia was tempting to the older boys of the Adams household, and she was always fending off their persistent advances. She sought refuge by hiding next door and wiling away the hours listening to Tituba's tales of far-away islands and the great mysteries of life. On one of her visits, Lydia saw that eighteen-year-old Nathan Parris was eavesdropping. It struck her that, even though he was listening to the sordid tales of Tituba, he nevertheless kept his eyes fixated on Lydia herself.

On subsequent visits, she asked Tituba about Nathan. Tituba arranged for them to visit alone. It wasn't long before they fell in love despite the fact that Nathan Parris' father, the Reverend Parris, would never condone such an eventual marriage, not to mention the other *activities* in which the two were oft engaging.

What began as simple looks and glances grew into lustful encounters of wanton passion. On leaving the two alone, Tituba invariably laughed as she closed the door. Nathan reached under Lydia's skirts and fondled her where she was laden with desire. She moaned and opened her bodice to reveal what his young mouth yearned for. Her firm and shapely breasts stood erect and were soaked with his kisses. In no time, he dropped his trousers and entered her. Invariably, Tituba admonished them to restrain their noisy heaving for fear of their being caught. Surely such a discovery meant a whipping for her at the hands of Reverend Parris as his church would not abide by such scandalous goings on. Sometimes, Tituba peeked through a crack in the door and watched the young lovers go at one another.

Lydia and the young Master Parris were in the third week of their affair when his younger sister woke the house with wretched screaming and strange utterances. Reverend Parris, shocked at the blasphemy coming from the mouth of his nine-year-old daughter, summoned Tituba. Beneath the bed of the slave, the lovers hid, naked and shaking out of utter terror that they would be discovered.

As his father pulled Tituba by the arm as he ascended the staircase that lead to the upstairs rooms, the younger Parris pulled Lydia from under the bed and helped her to her feet. Her body, aglow in the dim light of a single candle and ripened with the fullness of post-adolescence, looked irresistible. Nevertheless, he had to ignore her. He implored her to dress quickly and then return home as soon as she could get away undetected. He put on his own nightshirt and tiptoed back to his room.

In all of the excitement of his brothers and sisters running around the upstairs, no one noticed his absence. Tituba managed to subdue young Betty. When Nathan saw his father and asked what was going on. His father started to ask where he had been but was distracted by what he witnessed. The elder Parris simply told Nathan to return to his room and say nothing. Nathan readily obeyed and jumped into his bed. As he lay there thinking of how close he came to being caught, he wondered what was wrong with little Betty. Thoughts of Lydia then entered his mind and he fell asleep, smiling and wanting her to be next to him.

Chapter 10

Within the contemporary mind of the seventeenth century, the threat of witchcraft and demonic possession was as real as those of disease or famine. Though difficult for societies subsequent to the 1690's to consider, religion was the dominant force in every facet of their workaday lives. This is not to say that such people were without sin, as indeed they were not; but the ideas of predestination and forbearance were central tenants to the Puritans of Massachusetts and, therefore, sin was a threat to communal harmony and individual salvation.

Ideas and beliefs contrary to Puritan dogma were thought to be seditious as well as heretical. While cases of rival sects or denominations within Christianity brought banishment, such as in the case of Roger Williams' separatist movement during the 1630's, more extreme cases of witchcraft and demonic possession resulted in capital punishment. Serious sins, such as adultery or fornication, could result in public humiliation, corporeal punishment or permanent banishment. Drunkenness or singing in public could easily be considered as witchery and result in flogging, time in the pillory or outright incarceration.

Such consequences certainly hadn't escaped the minds of young Nathan Parris and Lydia Thorn. Nathan's relatively higher profile, being the son of a minister, posed greater-than-normal risks for the reputation of his family. Lydia, being an indentured servant to the Adams, risked scorn being brought upon herself as well as her employers. Public disclosure of her relationship with Nathan Parris would surely bring on the lash and the perpetual identity of a whore. Tituba, being a slave, would face severe punishment for being a mere accomplice to the fact.

As often in the case of youth, passion took precedence over discretion and romance refocused the minds. In the case of the young lovers, separated as they were by social positioning, they endured the threat of consequence in order to satiate their aching hearts. With only two years left to her indentureship, they could have waited for Lydia's standing to be upgraded and marry in a more acceptable state. Sadly, but altogether most assuredly, impatience on the part of the young lovers would prove to play a hand in their own undoing and therefore was the greatest sin that the two could commit.

United in love yet separated in fact, the lovers greeted the morning apart from one another. In the suitor's household, tense silence about the screaming of his younger sister was the order of the day. No one in the Parris' house spoke. The quiet was unnerving and the family did not partake much of the morning meal. Oddly, though unbeknownst to the Parrises, a similar set of circumstances beset their cousins' household next door.

Lydia began the day, much as she did every day, by sweeping the hearth with a broom she brought with her from London. It was her only possession given to her by the father that sold her into the indentureship five years prior. She did not resent her father for this because, as things were, he was unable to feed her siblings and it was this broom that her father gave her as a pitiful remembrance. The broom was, indeed, her *only* possession as she stepped ashore in the New World to begin seven years of service to Mr. Adams who financed her passage.

After sweeping the ashes and soot, she prepared the morning meal by building a fire from the embers that glowed within. Mrs. Adams asked her about the restless night that Abigail endured but Lydia had been elsewhere and knew nothing about it. For Mrs. Adams' sake, however, she told the woman that she was sleeping heavily and did not hear a thing.

Following the prayer led by Mr. Adams, the family, including Abigail, said nothing as they sat down to eat. It was a strangely daunting silence that gripped the family. The clanking of utensils and dishes seemed louder than normal, in the face of such quiet surroundings. Lydia went about her duties while mindful of her place. It wasn't as if she needed to arouse suspicions, in her own right, for she was aware that any investigation into her own behavior might reveal her relationship with the young man living next door.

That night, rather than risk discovery, Nathan told Tituba to get word to Lydia to stay home. It was wise and fortunate that he did this, for that night also brought on more screechings and incantations from the two girls. Betty and Abigail screamed and ranted at the same moment even though they were each in their own homes. It was loud enough to bring on the night watchman who subsequently informed the constable. Unfortunately, there could be no more silence to follow. The following morning brought on the full force of colonial law within the heart of Salem. Under subsequent questioning, Abigail revealed what Tituba told them about witchcraft and hexes. After repeated lashings at the hands of Reverend Parris, Tituba revealed this and more. Along with Betty and Abigail, Lydia Thorn found herself under arrest on the incredible charge of being a witch.

Chapter 11

Nathan Green never saw a table set the way Mrs. Wood set her table. Imported china from England and the finest silver and pewter from Boston were complemented by full lead crystal that must have come from Paris. He thought to himself, *what am I supposed to do with all of these forks and spoons?*

Carefully and cautiously, he watched others to see which implements they used for a given course, and then followed in the same manner as when apes imitate the actions of humans. His deception worked for the most part, but Anne noticed his apparent imitation and it amused her to watch this awesome physical specimen so terrified of making a mistake at the table set before them. His only gaffe was when he was asked by the waiter, an elderly black man affectionately referred to by the family as Spoons, if he would like more claret. He answered that he had quite enough on his plate, which aroused Lieutenant Wood's hearty laughter along with the rest of his family. The one who was *not* amused was Nathan. His face reddened upon the laughter from the others, and he felt stupid for his ignorance and the way in which he divulged this ignorance. He smiled tightly, looked over at Anne and noticed her staring at him. Her eyes sparkled with the reflection of the flame from the candle, and she was gazing directly into his eyes. If only he was alone with her at this moment, he would grab her and kiss her and squeeze her with all the pent-up desire his two dozen years had spawned.

When at last they were finished with dinner, Lieutenant Wood invited Nathan into the drawing room for brandy and cigars. The two men knew what the topic of conversation would be and yet stumbled for ways to begin the discussion they both, for vastly different reasons, dreaded. Finally, Lieutenant Wood began.

"Nathan, you've been milling around this house for two years …" Nathan was devastated at such an opening statement, "… and it hasn't always been for reasons that are related to business. It's quite obvious that there's something of the heart that exists between you and my daughter, which for the life of me, I cannot understand. Nor, for that matter, deny."

"Lieutenant —" Nathan attempted to interject.

"Nathan, *please* let us continue." He drew long on his cigar. "It is obvious that you wish to ask for Anne's hand, and it is with some misgivings that I would lend my consent. I want my daughter to be happy and yet I want her to marry into a good family."

"Lieutenant …" Nathan again made the attempt.

"Please Sergeant Green allow us to continue. I wasn't too impressed with your father's refusal to join us in our fight with King George. In fact, I despised him for his stubbornness. Ordinarily, sons must bear the sins of their fathers and, of course, there is the matter of one's class."

"Lieutenant …" Nathan attempted for a third time.

"Let us continue man … *for the love of it!*" Lieutenant Wood was growing impatient with the incessant attempts at interruption. "I have seen the dedication of your efforts when on maneuvers with the Militia, and it was for this that I recommended your promotion. I am prepared therefore, to overlook the actions of your father during the War. There is still the matter of class and although that too is a barrier with which we, in part, fought to overcome, I —"

"Lieutenant —" Nathan tried again.

"Be silent, man! I just want my Anne to be happy. I'm not thrilled at the prospect of her marrying a farmer. However, I also know from the way she looks at you that she'll be miserable if I do not give my consent. Now what is it that you feel you have to say?"

"Lieutenant Wood," Nathan stumbled briefly. "Lieutenant Wood it is true that my father chose not to fight in the war but, let me assure you, it was for reasons he felt strongly about. It wasn't that he supported the king. In fact, far from it. He just wanted to live his own life in his own way; that's all. Now you've also touched on the issue of class, sir. True, I am not a man of great means. I'm not in possession of luxuries to be sure." He gulped the brandy. "However, one of the many things that my father did teach me was the value of hard work. So help me, sir, as long as I have breath in my body your daughter will not know hunger. I'll care for her so that you'll not have to worry."

"I know you will Nathan. That is why I am consenting to this marriage." Lieutenant Wood spoke softly.

Nathan stood to shake the hand of his would-be father-in-law. In doing so, his legs hit the tea table which fell to the floor.

"Good God son ... that doesn't mean you can destroy my house in the process."

Nathan reached down to return the table to its place. He shook the hand of Lieutenant Wood, and the two burst into laughter.

"Thank you, sir. You'll not be sorry." Nathan offered.

"Not be sorry? I already am ..." The two men laughed again. "I'll fetch Anne. I suppose the two of you have a lot to talk about. Just don't break anything." He turned and left the room.

Nathan was beside himself. He did not even have to ask the question. While he waited for what seemed an eternity, he reached beneath his shirt and removed a chain. On it was the diamond ring his father once gave to his mother. He would soon offer it to Anne as a token of his promise.

At last she entered the room and sat on the edge of a chair near the table, which earlier had crashed to the floor. Nathan approached gingerly, fell to one knee and said, "Miss Wood … uh … Anne. I spoke to your father and he will allow me to ask for your hand. All I do know is that I love you and want to marry you. Will … will you marry me?"

Anne paused, looked at him as if she were staring right through him and replied, "Yes Nathan. I will be your wife."

He then kissed her with all of passions surging within the confines of his throbbing heart. Opening his eyes, he noticed she was crying.

"What's wrong Anne?"

"I've been waiting so long for you to ask that I wondered if you ever would." She sobbed. "Oh Nathan." The two embraced and their lips met again. Her tears soaked his cheek. She then pushed him away. "I must tell Mother. Please wait." She rose from the chair, turned around and left the room.

A few minutes passed when Lieutenant Wood returned. He smiled at Nathan and stepped closer.

"Nathan did you …?"

"Yes sir." Nathan sniffed.

"And did she?"

"She said yes." Nathan grinned.

"As well as I thought she would Sergeant. Congratulations son."

"Thank you, sir." Nathan smiled at Lieutenant Wood.

"I've spoken with Mrs. Wood. She's upstairs crying like a baby. I suppose it's not easy to lose a daughter is it?"

"You're not losing a daughter, sir." Nathan protested. "She will *always* be your daughter."

Lieutenant Wood smiled at the young man, happy with what he just heard. He realized Nathan was a good man who was about to become his son-in-law. Proud of his consent to the union, he stood tall with his chest full. "Here Nathan have some more brandy."

"Thank you, sir. I believe I will." Nathan felt that he was the luckiest man in the world.

The door to the drawing room opened and the mother and daughter entered. Both were flushed from crying. The mother approached Nathan and kissed his cheek.

"Take good care of my daughter Nathan." She sobbed.

"Oh, I will Mrs. Wood," he replied.

"*If* you are so inclined," the mother said, "I would prefer you call me Mother from now on."

"Yes, Mother." He sensed that this meant a great deal to the woman although it was strange to call someone 'Mother.' He never knew his own mother, nor much about her, save for what little his father had told him. Now he was addressing a living person with that very name. The four stood together and Nathan beheld the woman who was soon to become his beloved wife. He scarcely believed it. He remembered the ring that he held.

All in all, it had been quite a day at that.

Chapter 12

Lydia Thorn sat alone in her dank cell, sorting things out. She was desperately in love with Nathan Parris, but now she was also in fear for her life. If convicted, she would surely meet the gallows.

Betty Parris, Abigail Adams and Tituba were all housed in adjacent cells. For they too were charged with witchcraft. Her surroundings, as were theirs, were dreadfully sparse. There was a latrine in the corner with unspeakable odors emitting into the musty air. With no fire for warmth, she trembled from the cold. The only light was coming from a small window — too small for a petite woman to squeeze through — escape was impossible. There was only a scattering of decaying straw tossed haphazardly and not even enough of that from which to make a bed.

Two days passed since her arrest when three elderly women entered her cell. They were from the church and, upon entry, told her to remove her clothing.

"Why should I do this?" she asked.

"Yours is not to ask why child," one of them replied. "Take off your clothes!"

Lydia reluctantly obliged. The old ladies set about examining her naked body for signs of being a witch. During the examination, she shivered from the cold while being poked and prodded. While there were no suspecting blemishes or marks to be found that would have otherwise provided evidence of witchcraft, they were able to determine that Lydia had indeed lost her virginity.

"Who have you fornicated with?" asked one of the elderly examiners.

Lydia refused to divulge the name of her lover. They would not have believed her anyway. The son of a minister had a reputation beyond doubt, but this was not the reason she refused to disclose Nathan's name. She simply did not want to make trouble for the young man she loved. Repeated inquiries as to his identity produced no response.

"She must have fornicated with Beelzebub!" said one of the other women.

"That is *not* true." Lydia protested.

"Then, tell us the name of your fornicator wench," said the third woman. Lydia shook her head. "Get your clothes on."

The three women left. Lydia shivered and sobbed as she dressed. The horrible examination of her breasts was bad enough. The probing of her rectum and vagina was an invasion that Lydia could not have imagined from three respectable ladies of the church. Although these women were acting upon the direction of the church elders and on orders from the constable, Lydia nevertheless felt violated and, for the first time in her life, dirty and ashamed.

She was dressed and still sobbing when a light shone at her door. Standing at the threshold was none other than the Reverend Parris. He was holding her broom. Startled, she sat on the edge of the bed but said nothing.

The reverend spoke softly. "Lydia it has been determined that you committed fornication with the devil."

"It's not true Reverend ... it's —"

"I know what *is* the truth girl," Reverend Parris continued. "Nathan told me everything once I told him of the findings of the church examiners. I suspected all along that something illicit was going on between the two of you. When I received the report of the examiners, I went to Nathan and he told me about the grave sins you and he have committed. I come now to offer you a chance to redeem your life and save your neck as well."

"What do I —?"

"Silence girl!" replied the minister. "There isn't much time. You must leave Salem at once, never to return for the rest of your miserable life. If you don't, I'll see to it that you hang with the rest of those witches."

"I'm *not* a witch."

"Say nothing, leave now and may God, in His infinite wisdom, have mercy on your horrible soul. You may be a common whore, but you are no witch. I just cannot have these people knowing that my own son is a whoremonger. That's why you must leave now. Tomorrow, they will find this cell empty. They will assume that as a witch, you used your magic to disappear. Leave now and live. If you return, you will meet your death. Follow me and be quiet about it."

She followed Reverend Parris to the edge of a thick forest. He pointed her in a southwesterly direction and told her to keep walking. He handed her the broom — the same broom she brought from London.

That was the last Lydia ever saw of Salem, Massachusetts, and the last she ever saw of her unfortunate lover. She had her life, thanks to the elder Parris, but little else as she wandered into the dark woods of Massachusetts. The night was filled with the echoes of beasts and perhaps wild Indians. She was alone and frightened and cold. Having no idea as to what would become of her, or where she would go, she walked on. She wondered what her own family, far away across the sea, was doing at precisely that moment. She consoled herself with the fact that, at least, her father didn't know what had become of her. Under the circumstances, it was best that he did not know.

Chapter 13

During the most temperate years, winter in New England was brutal. The winter of 1692 was, to be sure, no exception. The snow in Massachusetts fell deep and although the thick forest broke some of the howling wind and nothing thawed the air of its bitter chill.

It was a clear night when Lydia, armed with nothing except her broom and frock, set out on the journey to which Reverend Parris and fate condemned her. Since there was barely a new moon, it was exceedingly dark. The only light seemed to emanate from the snow-covered ground. She dared not light a fire for warmth, lest she might attract danger from man or beast. Her only hope was to keep walking in the direction to which he had pointed. Cold and exhausted, Lydia struggled to continue onward. She was barely able to accept that she just lost the one person she loved, and the events of the last few days were more than she could stand. With each step, the harsh memories of Salem grew ever more distant in her mind. The fear of the night and the evil that lurked within it, gradually took hold of this young woman. Slowly, she became a part of the trees and the snow around her. With only the stars flickering between the branches to guide her, she continued onward toward the southwest and into the destiny that awaited her.

Salem, Massachusetts woke the following morning to the incendiary rumors that a suspected witch vanished from her jail cell. Such an impossibility did much to lend credence to the feeling that witchcraft, indeed, took hold of their community. Reverend Parris, at the insistence of the church's elders, petitioned the constable to coordinate a search party. The fact that drifting snow covering her tracks meant that no sign existed indicating Lydia Thorn's escape route. This fanned the fires of suspicion all the more. By sundown, Salem was reeling with accusations, rumors and false witnesses. The constable was forced, against his better judgement, to petition Governor William Phips to appoint a tribunal to investigate the remaining charges against Tituba and the two girls, Abigail Adams and Betty Parris. Now frightened beyond all reason, the two girls went into shrieking fits of blasphemous rage. Unintelligible ranting was intertwined with accusations spreading in a haphazard and random way.

March of 1692 brought preliminary hearings. As a result of testimony from dozens of witnesses, formal indictments followed in short order. In May, Governor Phips appointed Judge William Stoughton to chair a special tribunal, which tried one-hundred and fifty women before the end of the year. Even Cotton Mather, whose book sparked this whole lurid and horrible unfolding of events, became dismayed with the death sentences that were ultimately handed down.

Nathan Parris, neither under indictment nor even suspicion, was senseless at the loss of his lover and went into a silence that remained with him for the rest of his life. He was overcome with fear of his father but also with what was alleged against his sister and cousin and, above all else, Lydia. Taken together, he merely could not stand the strain.

Sadly, while the world around him was torn asunder with hysteria, Nathan Parris fell into a silent shell, never to speak again. He lived the remainder of his life as a church custodian. Only Nathan and his father knew of Lydia's release that January evening in 1692. Both carried this secret to their graves.

Lydia Thorn collapsed in the woods seven miles from Salem. She slept most of the morning and awoke to a sick stomach. She cleaned her face with the cool wet snow and set about building a fire. Doing so was tedious work. First, she had to strike the fallen branches against a tree-trunks to remove the snow and ice. After igniting a small fire by rubbing sticks, she added larger pieces and, eventually, was able to warm herself. Even though she found herself situated alone, the sun's rays reflecting off the snow created a patchwork of blinding spaces that divided the darkened shadows. Now, she had to find a way to eat. Despite her nausea, she was beset with a ravenous appetite.

After a considerable search, she happened upon two ears of partially eaten corncobs. As they were evidently left by a wild deer or perhaps an Indian, she returned to the fire and warmed the frozen corn. Still exhausted and growing chilled, she decided to stay put for the remainder of the afternoon. She stood there, quietly attending to the fire and wondering what her next meal would be. Salem seemed as far away as England.

When the last of the sun's rays disappeared in the west, the wolves howling stirred the silence of dusk. She thought about abandoning her campfire, but its warmth was seductive and her exhaustion immobilizing. The fire blazed and she immersed herself in the flickering flames. Sensing that she was not alone, she stared into the shadows. The sensation grew with the darkening of the sky. Her clothing was soaked. Setting her broom in front of herself, she took off her frock and underclothing. With each layer removed, she somehow felt lighter and freer. Now, as her clothes hung on nearby limbs to be dried by the fire, Lydia stood before the flames as naked as in the moment of her birth.

Chapter 14

Lydia Thorn awoke completely naked and shivering. Her clothes were now dry. The fire was smoldering but not generating any degree of heat. She dressed and it was a relief to wear warm clothing. Bearing a pounding headache, she felt a little disoriented. Her stomach churned and she vomited. Gasping, she wiped her cheek with a handful of snow.

She glanced around. It was quiet in the forest. All she could hear was the sound of her beating heart. She bent over, picked up the broom and walked, once again, in the southwesterly direction.

In the distance, there was a clearing. Lydia continued to walk. When she arrived at the edge of a river, the sun was directly above her head. Across the water lay the bustling town of Boston. Standing near the shore, Lydia beckoned over a small sailboat. Startled to see a young woman in the wilderness, the lone pilot of the craft asked if she required assistance.

The young man repeatedly asked for her name and where she was from; but she remained silent. The cold breeze coming off of the river felt refreshing, but something about the water seemed ominous. It wasn't as though she feared water. She lived within sight of the Thames, as a young girl, and then crossed a great ocean at the age of eleven. Salem, being situated close to the Atlantic, made her quite accustomed to being near large bodies of water. Yet within the shimmering below, she sensed a great danger.

She thanked the young man for the crossing and gingerly stepped onto the distant shore. She took great care not to get her feet wet. Strange, having wet feet didn't seem to bother her before. Now however, it terrified her.

Making her way through the streets of Boston, she happened upon a fruit and vegetable vendor who was sorting carrots. He was discarding the older ones. She told the elderly man she had no money and was hungry. He handed her a dozen carrots. She politely nodded. Asking him where she might find work, he said nothing but pointed to a church. Perhaps he may have been unable to speak, Lydia wasn't sure and didn't care anyway. He watched as she walked past the church.

By nightfall, Lydia had traversed to the outskirts of town. She walked precisely southwest. She nibbled on the carrots. When she came upon an abandoned barn near the edge of a forest, she decided it was a good place to sleep. Twenty-two miles of walking, much of it in deep snow during the last forty-eight hours, took a toll on her legs. She snuggled on a stack of hay and fell into a deep sleep. As she slept, Lydia was clutching her broom. And in her sleep, she felt as though she was flying — flying high above the treetops.

In her dream, she flew to a clearing in the thickest part of a dense forest. There was a fire burning below and people were dancing in a circle. She landed on the ground and noticed that they were all women and nude. There was young Abigail Adams spinning and laughing alongside Betty Parris. There were other females, young and old, dancing around the blaze. Of these other women, she was only able to recognize Tituba. Her black breasts, swaying back and forth with her gyrations, reflected the light of the flames. Tituba reeled around, noticed Lydia, and laughed. Tituba's dark eyes looked as though they were on fire.

Tituba then froze as did the other women. All looked at Lydia and smiled. All had fire in their eyes. Tituba motioned Lydia to step forward.

The Broom

She found herself standing in the center with the fire to her back. She removed her clothes and placed them on the ground. She looked at Tituba whose eyes were now glaring and then glanced down at where she left her clothes. They were gone. In front of her was a sign drawn on the ground with ashes. It was a circle, inside of which, was a pentagram. At the center of the pentagram was a small cross, under which, were two wavy lines. Between the cross and the wavy lines was a black candle flickering a tiny flame. She knelt down before the sign and listened as Tituba cited the forbidden incantation summoning Diana — goddess of the hunt.

The incantation complete, Lydia lay on her back with her legs spread on either side of the sign. Betty Parris held her right ankle — Abigail Adams held her left. Two older women, whom she did not know, held her wrists. Her feet were at the edge of the fire's hot coals. Tituba held Lydia's broom. With a sudden thrust, the handle of the broom was inserted into Lydia's vagina and the women said in unison, "So be it."

Tituba withdrew the broom's handle, looked down at Lydia and said, "Now, you are one of us Lydia." The others, rejoicing, resumed their dance and soon Lydia found herself dancing along with them.

Lydia awoke the following morning with her head throbbing. She felt stiff as she rose and the area between her legs was sore. She bent over, picked up her broom and, on doing so, felt nauseous. For the third time in as many mornings, she vomited. Collapsing into the hay, she wondered what made her so sick and yet so hungry.

Chapter 15

As the weeks passed, Lydia Thorn continued her journey in a generally southwestern direction. When her abdomen swelled and the new life within moved, it became obvious that she was with child. As much as she might have wanted to return to her baby's father, doing so would have meant her quick demise. Bits and pieces of news from the trials found their way to Lydia, and this kept her on the constant move, ever more distant from Salem.

Although the dreams of Tituba and the others had not recurred, Lydia became cognizant of a growing awareness within herself. She became adept at sensing a different and new world of which she had not previously been made aware. As she came into contact with others, she sorted out those who were helpful from those who were not, which was of tremendous value to a young woman without the means to support herself. She also felt more a part of the natural world and less a part of humanity. She sensed a natural order and rhythm to the earth and came to consider people as something not of this world. She avoided the crowded villages and towns of New England and made her way toward the colonies of the Middle Atlantic.

By late September 1692, she settled into an abandoned cabin located in the Lehigh Valley of eastern Pennsylvania. As the leaves of the surrounding slopes turned to an autumnal brilliance, she realized that her time to give birth was near. In the dark of an early October night, the first of her labor pains hit. As the pains intensified, she relieved them by biting down on the handle of her broom. Lying on the dirt floor of a cabin, her labor pains grew. With a final thrust, she screamed and her baby, a boy, was born.

Without the help of anyone, she delivered her baby into the world. She was overwhelmed with a sense of despair. What was she going to do with a baby? She nursed the child and cared for it during the next couple of weeks but never acquired the maternal sense of bonding that is normal between a mother and her child. Well aware that her feelings toward the child would be of no benefit to him, she took him to a nearby cabin where a young couple and their two children lived.

On the night of October 31st, Lydia wrapped her unnamed baby in a deerskin and set it at the doorstep of the family she did not know. She knocked at the door with her broom handle and ran off into the night. From behind a shrub, she watched as the door opened. The man looked down at the crying baby, stepped carefully over it and peered into the darkness. His mouth hung in bewilderment. His wife, now holding the foundling infant in her arms, motioned him into the cabin and shut the door.

Satisfied that her baby was safe in the arms of a mother who would give him love, Lydia walked away with no regret. She intended to return to the cabin from whence she came, but never did. Onward, toward the southwest she traveled. By the dead of winter, Lydia crossed into Maryland.

Chapter 16

Nathan Green bade his fiancée farewell. They kissed one more time on the front steps of her father's home. He placed his mother's ring on the fourth finger of her left hand.

He mounted his recently acquired horse and set off for the home his parents had built. Isaac Green died almost six years prior to the engagement of his son and had left him the house and its surrounding land. Nathan thought about his father on his ride home, and although only a few miles, it somehow seemed to be longer than usual. Most of the days, during the next eight months, seemed to pass slowly to the young man who was to be married the following Christmas Eve. Not usually inclined to impatience, Nathan found himself wanting time to pass quickly. The more impatient he grew, the slower time seemed to pass by.

He already finished his spring planting when he asked for Anne's hand. Work in the fields kept Nathan occupied as the days grew ever longer and hotter. On Sunday afternoons, he ate dinner at the Woods, at their home. The six and one-half days in between those dinners were excruciating. Lieutenant Wood saw to it that the young lovers spent Sunday afternoons in the watchful presence of either himself, or else

Mrs. Wood. Lieutenant Wood remembered, all too well, the passions of youth.

During these visits, Nathan and Anne were only allowed a few moments alone … mostly on his departure following dinner, which served to make their passions ever more incendiary. During these brief interludes, they embraced closely and kissed deeply until Anne was summoned into the house. It became difficult for Nathan to mount his horse following these farewells. Often, he ambled away leading his horse by the reins until he calmed down and was able to mount. Little could he have imagined how her own heart pounded within the breast of his beloved. Only the change in her own complexion disclosed these feelings to Anne's mother who was quick to divert her daughter's attention with the subsequent assignment of a mundane domestic chore.

Nathan dreamed of his fiancée as he slept alone, often waking during the heat of arousal. Only after reading his mother's Bible or ciphering farm-related accounting in his head could he return to sleep. Farming aside, as far as he was concerned, Christmas could not arrive soon enough.

Chapter 17

By the time Lydia Thorn arrived at the rolling hills of Maryland, five decades of internal strife had come to an end. On the day he died, George Calvert (Lord Baltimore), a Roman Catholic of immense wealth, was granted by King Charles I proprietary rights to the lands north of the Potomac and up to Pennsylvania's southern border — a border which later would be firmly established by the survey of Charles Mason and Jeremiah Dixon, in the following decades. The grant included all of the Potomac and ended on Virginia's shore. Calvert's son, Cecilius, thus became Maryland's first proprietor who then dispatched two hundred colonists — half of them also Catholic — to this region under the auspices of following the tenants of the Church, and without interference from government. Since the concept of religious freedom was at the heart of the colony's founding, the Toleration Act of 1649 was passed in the Maryland colonial legislature so as to ensure this freedom to Protestants and Catholics, alike. Within five years however, Protestants had seized effective control of the colony and subsequently outlawed 'practices relating to the Popery or Prelacy.' The ensuing decades saw power shift back and forth amongst the opposing forces until 1691, when the former proprietary colony became a royal colony directly under the auspices of the sovereign king, William II and his queen, Mary II.

Lydia Thorn arrived in Maryland eighteen months afterwards and, although it was January, she noticed it was not nearly as cold as it had been in New England. Arriving at a house on the headwaters of the Patapsco River, she knocked at its door intending to ask for something to eat. There was something about the house that gave her the sense that she would be welcomed by those who lived there.

The door swung open and a middle-aged man addressed her as if he expected her arrival. He was in a state of distress and pulled her inside. Lydia discovered the reason for his erratic behavior. On the bed lay a woman, presumably his wife, thrashing about with labor pains.

"I don't know what to do," he said.

Lydia did not answer, but went to the woman, instead. She put her hands on the woman's abdomen. Lydia lifted the woman's skirts and pulled off the undergarments. The baby's head was crowning. The woman was in agony. Lydia, placing the broom handle in the woman's mouth, said, "Bite down and push!"

"I can't," gasped the woman.

"Do as I say now!" Lydia snapped.

The woman did so.

"We're almost there." Lydia's voice was now more comforting to reassure the woman.

Another pain hit and the woman pulled the broom handle back to her mouth. Lydia placed her hands around the baby's head as it came. Another push and the shoulders appeared. The baby slipped into Lydia's awaiting arms.

"Don't just stand ye' by," Lydia yelled at the husband. "Get me a knife and twine."

The man gave a knife to Lydia. She cut the umbilical cord. She then tied the cord's stump closed with the twine.

"Now bring me something to wipe this child off."

The man obeyed and handed Lydia some rags.

"Water!" Lydia's voice was stern.

Again, the man fetched a pail of water and returned.

"Soak the rags, ring 'em out and hand 'em to me."

Carefully, Lydia took the soaked rags and wiped the fluids from the baby. It cried from the shock of the cold water. She wrapped the child in a blanket and told the man to place a pillow behind the mother's back. The father did as he was told.

Lydia softened her voice. "This girl is hungry. You must feed her."

The woman opened her blouse and Lydia placed the baby onto the bed. As the mother watched her daughter suckle, Lydia reeled around and resumed her harsh tone.

"You help your wife for a few days," she said. "Change these bed linens. I'll wipe down your wife. Get me something to eat."

Once again, the man did precisely as instructed. After a while he returned and said, "There's a plate of food on the table."

"Get this bed cleaned while I eat." Lydia did not waver from her harsh tone.

The man did not protest, for it was obvious that this strange woman had fortuitously arrived. Furthermore, she was of immense help at a time when he was without the knowledge or skills needed to assist. Cautiously, the man removed the soiled linens from beneath his wife and replaced them with clean ones. The baby was asleep having been adequately fed. He told his wife that she too should get some rest while he chopped wood for the fire.

Upon leaving the house, the new father noticed that the stranger who came to their rescue was sitting at the table eating. He went on to chop wood taking up his axe and thrusting the blade into the hard, white oak. He grunted, yet continued, until he had a sufficient armful. Opening the door, he immediately dropped the pieces of wood directly onto the coals. He poked at the logs and a flame kicked up. He watched the flame as it grew.

He went to his wife and new baby. Peacefully and silently, they slept from the exhaustion of the day. He stood by the bed and watched for a short while. His eyes flooded with tears when he noticed how calmly the mother and her daughter slept beside one another.

It then occurred to him that he hadn't properly thanked the strange woman who so adeptly averted what might have been a disaster. Walking back toward the table where she was eating, he said, "I wanted to thank you for …" He stopped himself short. The stranger was gone with only an empty plate left behind.

Chapter 18

Lydia Thorn was living in Maryland when she passed her eighteenth year in 1694. She enjoyed the milder climate and the gentle breezes that descended from the Chesapeake Bay. Political squabbling between Catholics and Protestants enabled her to fade into the background, compared to what took place in Massachusetts. There simply was no preoccupation with witchcraft in Maryland.

Still careful not to foster acquaintance, her abilities as a midwife became something of legend to the planters and watermen who lived along the streams and rivers of Maryland's western shore. She acquired a knack for showing up precisely at the crucial moment when a woman needed her most. She was occasionally rewarded for her assistance. Most people surmised that she must have heard of their specific needs from others living nearby. Avoiding lengthy conversation, her knowledge of women in such circumstances might otherwise have proved to be impossible. Having gone through the birth of her own child, all alone and afraid, Lydia became sympathetic toward women who were in labor. Such an ability to seek and find these women, right at the opportune time, was something she just *sensed*.

As the seventeenth century passed into the eighteenth, Lydia was now in her twenty-fifth year. Yet she still looked identical to the young woman Reverend Parris escorted out of Salem eight years prior. Opportunities to gaze at herself in a mirror were seldom and she regarded mirrors with disdain. The fact remained that, despite the hardships of childbirth, a lengthy journey on foot and incessantly staying on the move, Lydia Thorn's body was no worse for the wear. She simply wasn't aging the way other women aged under similar circumstances.

After she delivered a fisherman's firstborn son and, having been rewarded with a plate of roasted oysters, Lydia was walking along a path that paralleled the western shore of the Chesapeake Bay. Looking down, she noticed a strange pattern that seemed both oddly, and yet ominously, familiar. She stared intently at the five-pointed star etched in the sand. The points were joined by a surrounding circle. Within the central pentagon of the star was a cross and two wavy lines. A chill ran down her back. She nervously glanced around making sure no one else was nearby. She promptly swept the pattern from the sand with her broom.

"Tituba! … she knows I am here and there's something she wants."

She wondered as to what strange fate allowed Tituba to escape the gallows and by what stranger fate Tituba managed to follow her so far from Salem.

"Why is she just now making her presence known?"

Lydia traveled nearly ten miles inland from the shores of Chesapeake Bay when she finally arrived at Fells Point. She followed the dusty streets toward the wharf and noticed a medium-sized boat, which was being readied to set sail across the northwest branch of the Patapsco River.

"Kind sir," she called out to the captain. "Are you going to the south shore?"

"Why do you ask?" grumbled the captain.

"Perhaps you could take me aboard. Just as far as it takes to get across sir."

"Very well. Get in and be quick about it." The captain did not change his tone.

The south shore was a small peninsula, which divided the northwest and middle branches of the Patapsco River. Within two decades, the villages of Fells Point, Falls Town (named for Jones Falls) and the wharves on the harbor's western side would be incorporated to form the bustling town of Baltimore, named for the Calverts' estate along the coast of southern Ireland. At the time Lydia was making her crossing, only Fells Point was in existence and yet was a thriving tobacco port.

On the peninsula was a plantation owned by Andrew Sean McComas. The McComas plantation was quite large. McComas's father was indentured to a Virginia planter. Being Catholic, he was not permitted to own land in Virginia. Therefore, he made his way north to Maryland as soon as his indentureship was completed. Settling at Locust Point, he cleared the land between two branches of the Patapsco River where he planted tobacco. He saved enough money to purchase two Negro slaves, one man and one woman who together bore four children — three of them boys. By the time the elder McComas died leaving the large estate to his eldest son, a full dozen slaves worked at the Locust Point Plantation. Two of the twelve slaves were women. In addition to the remaining ten who worked as field hands, there were also four children all of whom were the offspring of one of the two enslaved women.

In the year before Lydia arrived, Andrew McComas took a wife who was now about to give birth to their first child. As was what had become more than usual, Lydia stepped ashore just minutes before the child first saw this world. When one of the slaves ran to tell the captain that Mrs. McComas was about to give birth, Lydia sped off toward the large house at the top of the hill.

She entered and went directly upstairs to Mrs. McComas's bedchamber. Lying on the bed was the lady of the house in the throes of heavy labor. Lydia instructed her to bite down on the handle of the broom and went to work.

On finishing, she was asked by Mr. McComas to see Hattie, the cook, about getting something to eat. Lydia entered the kitchen and sat down. Before Lydia could even speak, the cook turned around. Lydia gasped.

"Lydia, child," Tituba grinned, "it's been a *lo-ong* time …"

Chapter 19

George Washington completed his first year as President of the United States when his trusted lieutenant, Josiah Wood, announced the engagement of his daughter, Anne, to a Sargent Nathan Green of the Virginia Militia. Writing to his former commander in the field, Lieutenant Wood addressed the president as General:

Wood's Mill,
Nelson County, Virginia
May 1st, A.D. 1790

My Dear General,

It is with great pleasure that news of your being selected as President of the United States has reached your faithful Lieutenant. As I hope and pray, this letter finds the General and Mrs. Washington in good health. It is my honour to announce the engagement of my eldest daughter, Anne, to Sergeant Nathan Green of the Virginia Militia. Although he is neither an officer nor a man of considerable wealth, he is a fine young gentleman and a good soldier.

As I am inclined to appreciate the burdens of your office, realizing that I am asking something of my commanding general which he may not be in a position to grant, I therefore humbly request the honour of your presence at the marriage of my daughter on the eve of Christmas next.

As I send kindest regards to Mrs. Washington, I remain, sir,

> Your obedient servant,
> Lieutenant Josiah Wood

Twenty weeks later, Lieutenant Wood received the following reply:

Executive Mansion
City of New York
July 10th, AD 1790

My Dear Lieutenant,

It is with great happiness that I am in receipt of your letter of May 1st, announcing the engagement of your daughter. Mrs. Washington and I pass along our good wishes and tidings to you, Mrs. Wood, Sergeant Green, and the future Mrs. Green.

As debate continues over the establishment of a National Bank, with no indication from Congress of an imminent settlement, I should regret having to respectfully decline your gracious invitation. It seems that Congress would deprive its president of returning to his beloved Mount Vernon, as well.

Please extend my regrets to Mrs. Wood, as also to your daughter and her fiancé. I remain,

> Your obt. srvt.,
> George Washington

Disappointed that the affairs of state would preclude his general (and president) from attending the wedding of his daughter, Lieutenant

Wood realized he had to break the news to Anne who hadn't seen General Washington since being bounced on his knee, twelve years before, and was so counting on his presence.

Anne and her mother spent the summer planning the wedding that would take place on Christmas Eve at their home. Letters of correspondence were written and sent. The mail was slow and the process of waiting for replies was excruciatingly long. Since Anne was all of six inches taller than her mother and her full breasts larger, there was no way she could fit into her mother's wedding gown. In August, the satin and lace arrived. Mrs. Wood would make her daughter's dress. Advice from the ladies of neighboring farms, though not always welcomed and even less frequently sought, was nonetheless forthcoming. Mrs. Wood had quite a reputation as to her own skill with needle and thread. No doubt, this would be a stunning and elegant bridal gown and would take more than a month to complete.

Lieutenant Wood and Sargent Green were away on maneuvers during the latter part of August and early September. The constant threat of Indian uprising, though on the considerable wane, was at the time still very much on the minds of white Virginians. It was imperative that a well-trained and outfitted militia be at the ready just in case.

On the second Sunday of September, the two men returned to the women who awaited them. Lieutenant Wood didn't mind that his daughter and her fiancé kissed one another in full view of himself and his wife. The four joined Anne's younger sisters for a homecoming feast of pheasant, sweet potatoes, butter beans and white corn. Delicious apple pie was the dessert. Nathan remembered this as the best meal he'd ever had.

After they finished eating, Nathan asked Lieutenant Wood if he and Anne might go for a short walk. The lieutenant consented admonishing the two youngsters not to be gone too long. At last, Nathan was able to spend some time alone with the woman he had so dearly missed. As they walked toward the edge of the Rockfish River, the sun rested on Devil's Knob and the sky was afire in the light of late-summer dusk.

Chapter 20

It had been almost nine years since Lydia had last seen Tituba. Remarkably, Tituba looked quite the same as Lydia remembered. Her apparent age could have been anywhere between twenty and fifty. No one in Salem was ever quite certain. As Tituba ladled stew into a pewter bowl, she told Lydia to sit down 'a spell' and listen to what she was about to say.

Tituba began by recounting what she knew of the events concerning the trials. In March of 1692, preliminary trials were held. Tituba, although a slave and not considered a subject of the Crown in the same sense as a white woman, was ordered to testify before the tribunal as to her involvement with Betty Parris and Abigail Adams. During the course of this inquiry, it became apparent that the only way she could save her own neck was by confessing that she was, indeed, Satan's servant. Under testimony, she related stories of witchcraft, hexes and magic to the young girls in order that she might gain additional minions to do his bidding. Furthermore, she was forced to admit that Lydia was a witch who used her magic powers to escape the cell that imprisoned her.

To Lydia's astonishment, Tituba related the rest of the grizzly facts to her. A total of nineteen men and women were hung, while another was slowly pressed to death under the weight of boulders. Lives were ruined and innocent people were banished for good. For her own part in the proceedings, Tituba's life was spared under the condition that Reverend Parris would sell her south and thereby banish her from New England. Being the Puritan that he was, he jumped at the chance to sell her to a Papist living in Maryland and, in doing so, told Mr. McComas that her name was Hattie. For the last seven years, she'd been living here at Locust Point.

Lydia was shocked to find that all of these innocent people were executed while the perpetrator was spared. Terrified at the treachery of Tituba, Lydia went out of her way to appear sympathetic. Tituba did not know what ever became of Nathan Parris. Lydia felt it best not to disclose to her the birth of their son.

However, Lydia did ask about the sign she found along the beach at Edgemere. Tituba then finally admitted she was, in fact, a witch.

"A witch can assume the form of a rat, a cat or a puff of smoke," Tituba said.

Lydia wasn't sure whether to believe her or not. At an instant, Tituba disappeared leaving Lydia alone in the kitchen. A black cat leapt into Lydia's lap, looked up at her and meowed.

Lydia gasped. "Is that you Tituba?"

The cat jumped onto the floor and stepped over to where Tituba had been standing. In a blink of an eye, Tituba stood staring at Lydia. Tituba laughed. "Do you believe me now?"

Lydia was speechless. She tepidly nodded.

"I escaped Locust Point by nightfall, because I knew you was nearby."

"How?" Lydia asked.

"I sat on my broom and concentrated precisely on where I wanted to go."

"You flew on a broom?"

"That's what witches do. I flew to Edgemere and left you a message in the sand where you found it."

Lydia nodded. Lydia was confused. "How did you know I would find it?"

Tituba laughed again. "All witches communicate to fellow witches through our minds. We call it the Covenant of the Circle. Within a circle, witches are not bound by time."

"Time?"

Tituba shook her head. "Concentrate. And with your broom, you travel through time or across the land. The only limitation to such travel is the span of a witch's own lifetime. A witch's life is longer than mortals ... if we're not killed first. We live about a hundred and twenty-five years."

Lydia sat speechless listening to Tituba's strange talk. Since witches worshipped Diana, the goddess of the hunt, they spent their lives as humans searching for converts, concocting potions, casting spells and doing magic. On dying, those who spent lifetimes as witches hunting for converts are reincarnated as the hunted — a deer, a fox, a bear, etc.

"Given all these powers," Lydia asked, "then what is there to fear?"

"Water!" Tituba screeched. "It's fatal for a witch to be dunked into water and judged at the same time."

"What about the Blessed Sacrament?" Lydia asked. "Catholics live here."

"Coming into contact with the Host is the same as being dunked in water ... Catholics? There ain't no better cover than to live among such people ... they ain't crazy about witchcraft like they is in Salem." Tituba let out a loud and retched laugh. "I'm never asked to attend their services. Catholics are cautious when practicing their magic."

Lydia's eyes widened.

The Host ... at that time in colonial Maryland, it was against the law for Catholics to celebrate Mass. They were sporadically, but repeatedly restricted until the Constitutional ratification in 1788.

"Then why didn't you leave Salem before the trials?"

Tituba frowned. "I did not have access to my broom."

"You could have changed into a cat and looked for it."

"No child," Tituba said. "In order for a witch to change we must be near our broom."

So, that was that. Tituba was a witch. Lydia reflected. "What about other powers?"

"Witches are from the Earth. Since we're more Earth than mortal, we're in tune with nature. Witches do not desire the attention of our Heavenly Host. We are unencumbered by the constraints of Christian morality. Our senses, such as predicting weather or foretelling an impending birth, are just some of our gifts."

Everything was starting to make sense now. Lydia began to understand why she was able to happen upon women just at the moment they were about to give birth … and why she was so terrified of the river. It now occurred to her that she, herself, was a witch …

Chapter 21

Lydia sat in the McComas' kitchen thinking about what she learned.

A witch? she said to herself. Lydia looked over at Tituba and took in a deep breath. "How?"

"How what, child?" replied Tituba.

"How is it I became a witch?" Lydia frowned.

"You don't remember do you?" Tituba smiled.

"Remember what?" Lydia squinted her eyes.

"I scarcely remember myself. I still remember how it felt when the broom handle ... when I was initiated. Always seems like a dream."

"You assaulted me with a broom?" Lydia gasped.

"Not *a* broom." Tituba laughed. "*Your* broom ... and don't use the word assault. With *your* broom, we consummated you into our coven. That's how you became one of us child."

"One of who?" Lydia asked.

"The coven." Tituba huffed. "Aren't you listening, child? You're a part of our coven now."

That horrible dream. It was not a dream at all. It happened. Tituba was explaining everything in explicit detail. Tears welled in Lydia's eyes.

"Relax child." Tituba smiled. "It's not so terrible being a witch. Look at the good you did upstairs ... Mrs. McComas."

"What if I don't want to make others a witch?" Lydia protested.

"Then you'll break your chain." Tituba shook her head.

"What chain?"

"Your chain ... your line. I am your mother witch. I initiated you. The woman in Jamaica who initiated me is your grandmother witch and so on and so on."

"And what if I break this chain?"

"Then it's broken. That is all." Tituba huffed again. "You're a witch. It's up to you whether to continue your chain. Live out your life as you wish. We have good witches and bad witches. Which one you are is up to you."

A tear ran down Lydia's cheek.

"It's important you recognize the powers you possess. And how you use them."

Lydia allowed herself to be taken in by Tituba. Her words were indeed intoxicating, partially because she was tired from such a long walk and then learning so much about being a witch, all in the same day.

"Hattie?" the voice of Mr. McComas echoed through the room.

"Yessah Mr. McComas," hollered Tituba. "I's a-comin'."

She whispered to Lydia, "Stay here child and sleep ... we'll talk more in the mornin' ... just rest now, ya' hear?"

Lydia was too exhausted to say otherwise. Within minutes of Tituba leaving, Lydia fell asleep as she sat in the chair facing the fire.

Chapter 22

Tituba fixed things for Lydia. As fate would have it, Mrs. McComas agreed for Lydia to remain as hired help. With her difficult pregnancy (twice she came close to miscarriage) and then her own trouble giving birth to this newborn, Mrs. McComas was sorely in need of extra help. As things were her post-partum convalescence took several weeks, so Lydia was duly employed and was referred to as *Nurse Thistle* — an intentional pseudonym of *Hattie's* creation. This was employed just in case a warrant was circulated along the shores of the Patapsco for one *Lydia Thorne*.

Mr. McComas was delighted with the woman who helped his wife bear him a son. He already relied upon Hattie's in-depth knowledge regarding the state of his wife's condition. When Hattie suggested that Lydia remain, Mr. McComas was most agreeable. In exchange for her services, Lydia was given a room and a stipend of five shillings per week. It was *more* than Lydia could ever ask for.

In addition to caring for Mrs. McComas, Lydia's responsibilities included tending to the needs of the newborn. During the next several weeks, her days were filled with diapering, bathing and bringing young Sean to Mrs. McComas for feeding. When she wasn't busy with the baby, Lydia helped Mrs. McComas out of and back into her bed.

Five weeks passed before Mrs. McComas was able to descend the stairs. Soon and with Lydia's help, Mrs. McComas was able to eat her meals at the family table. Her overall mood significantly improved. When she dressed in something other than a nightgown, her spirits soared.

Mrs. McComas soon tended to young Sean herself. At first, she carefully noted how Lydia diapered and bathed him. Then under watchful instruction took on her own maternal responsibilities. As the spring passed into summer, Mrs. McComas began all of her regular errands, which included weekly day-long trips across the river to Fells Point. On these days, Lydia remained behind with Sean while his mother busied herself at the market. By mid-summer, Lydia's sole responsibility was to baby-sit Sean on market days much to the frugal dismay of Mr. McComas. Room, board and five shillings per week were not so dear for a nurse, but quite another matter for just a babysitter whose regimen was limited to but one day in every seven. Grudgingly and with spoken stubbornness, he acquiesced to the whining demands of his wife.

Summer passed into autumn as Lydia spent her eighth month at Locust Point. Sean was a healthy child, and Lydia soon became attached to the boy. Sometimes, she played with him on the days Mrs. McComas was at home, and she looked forward to market day when she had Sean all to herself.

October was magnificent on Locust Point. The skies were bluer than in summer, and the river, which flowed to nearby Chesapeake Bay, took on a sapphire hue. Lydia never knew such beauty in all of her twenty-five years. That summer for the first time, she tasted a delicacy known to locals as steamed crabs. Although not as succulent as the oysters of autumn, she became quite fond of picking the contents from the intricate carapace of a blue crab steamed red. Nothing save raw oysters, pleased her palate more than the white back fin meat thus rendered.

For the sake of convenience, she took to traveling on her broom, always careful to do so only at night, lest she be seen. Slightly bending her knees while standing, she held onto the broom. Placing the sturdy

The Broom

handle beneath her buttocks, she closed her eyes. She concentrated on her desired destination and suddenly became aloft.

With days spent with Sean and nights traveling in the air, sometimes with Tituba, Lydia had the time of her life. Once the McComas's were asleep, the two quietly left the house. Their destination always the same—due southeast to Sparrows Point, a small peninsula surrounded on three sides by the Chesapeake Bay. They joined other witches and danced naked around a bonfire while drinking a potent brew. Everything led to a huge celebration slated for the eve of All Hallows. October was coming to a close.

In order to celebrate Holy Mass on All Hallows Day, Mr. and Mrs. McComas left Locust Point early on the evening of October thirty-first. Anti-Catholic sentiment was on the upswing lately, and Mass was secretly held at dawn that following day, at the stately home owned by the Carroll family who lived to the north of Fells Point. Young Sean had a runny nose and Mrs. McComas thought it best to leave the boy with Lydia.

Tituba, treacherous to the core, tried to persuade Lydia to bring the boy along to the witches' sabbath. After much hesitation, Lydia relented to the unceasing petitions of Tituba. Wrapping the baby carefully in a warm blanket, Lydia set off for Sparrows Point with Sean securely in her right arm while holding onto the broom with her left.

When she arrived just after dusk, the fire was already blazing. Lydia set the baby wrapped in its blanket nearby. She wanted him to stay warm. She partook in two cups of brew and started dancing. Removing her dress and underclothing, she joined with the others in the dancing and celebrating as she had so often done in the evenings before. She kept a watchful eye on young Sean. He seemed to be greatly amused, watching all the naked women cavorting around the light of the fire.

When the women danced themselves into a frenzy, Tituba grabbed the baby and slew him with a knife before Lydia was able to stop her. Lydia screamed in horror at the lifeless child who she loved. The others laughed at her in derision. Lydia fell naked to the ground clutching the dead baby. She sobbed in wretched shock at what happened. As the others danced around her laughing, an uninhibited rage roared from somewhere deep inside Lydia. She gently placed the baby on the ground and pulled out the knife. She lunged at his wicked assailant. However, Tituba was too fast for Lydia and disappeared into a cloud of smoke. The others laughed even harder. One by one, she lunged at each, and as Tituba had, each disappeared into smoke just before the knife would have penetrated their torsos.

Lydia found herself alone standing in the glow of a bonfire. Holding the knife, she came very close to killing herself for she indeed felt culpable for the murder of this poor innocent boy. Momentarily, she took the knife and threw it into the fire. Getting dressed, she wrapped the lifeless baby in a blanket and set off on her broom for Locust Point.

In the family plot next to the remains of his very own grandfather, Lydia interred poor little Sean into a shallow grave. She wiped the dirt from her hands, sat upon her broom and, still crying, headed toward the southwest. Lydia never returned to the place she regarded as her home. She vowed not to associate herself with the practices relating to witchcraft, except for traveling by broomstick. She held close to this vow and kept that awful secret for the rest of her life.

Upon their return from the Carroll Mansion, Mr. and Mrs. McComas were shocked to say the least that their son — along with his babysitter — was missing. The constable at Fells Point was summoned. A search party formed and within an hour, a fresh grave in the family plot was discovered. The corpse of infant Sean McComas was exhumed and, having been found wrapped in a blanket, it became apparent that he was the victim of a knife wound to the heart. A warrant for Lydia Thistle was summarily issued and dispatched to all persons living in the colony of Maryland.

Tituba, the homicidal maniac who ultimately committed the heinous murder of Sean McComas, remained at Locust Point pleading absolute ignorance of what had taken place. Along both shores of the Chesapeake Bay, and the many rivers flowing into it, word of the horrendous deed spread like wildfire. For a crime she did not commit, the name of Lydia Thistle came to be reviled as an evil murderer in the annals of colonial Maryland history.

Within a month of Sean's untimely death, Mrs. McComas was herself dead of a broken heart. On the first day of December, in the year 1701, Mrs. Mary Alicia McComas was laid to rest beside her only child. Mr. McComas wept bitterly while Father Carroll administered the burial rites of the Catholic Church. Speaking the words in Latin, he too cried. Everyone else in attendance cried except for one. Hattie, the family cook, stood silent and without expression. She knew of the horrendous evil she committed and felt secure in the knowledge of her true identity.

Chapter 23

For the second time within a decade, Lydia fell victim to the treachery of Tituba. She was blamed for a child's murder, a crime she did not commit, while the guilty party was exonerated of complicity. Since she was now a fugitive, Lydia had no choice but to cross the Potomac into Virginia. Perhaps there she could forge a new life among the tobacco planters who cultivated prosperity in its richly fertile soil.

She spent the next several months making her way due south until she arrived in the bustling capital of Colonial Virginia. During her journey to Williamsburg, she managed to help seven women give birth including a young Indian who wandered far from her tribe.

Arriving in Williamsburg in late May 1702, Lydia found the town to be a place of unbridled opportunity and tremendous activity. Four years earlier, fire had virtually destroyed the former capital of Jamestown, and Virginia's Burgesses, already weary of inherent problems associated with the mosquito-laden swamps surrounding Jamestown Island, seized upon the opportunity to relocate its seat of government. They arrived upon a site, some five miles inland, known as Middle Plantation. Chartered in 1699, and named for King William III, the fledgling town was laid out with its principal, mile-long thoroughfare honoring the

Duke of Gloucester. At the western terminus of this broad street was the new College of William and Mary named for the King and Queen of England. At the street's eastern end lay the site of the new capitol building.

During the time of Lydia's arrival, this legislative building was under construction. Its design was purported to be the brainchild of Sir Christopher Wren, or perhaps of James Gibbs, his talented understudy. The building featured two three-story wings that were joined by a three-story connecting corridor. Its first story was complete and its second was well under way when Lydia first laid eyes on the enormous edifice. During her many years in Williamsburg, Lydia saw this project and many others completed.

She took a room above the Apothecary Shop and assisted the druggist in the preparations of elixirs. Her knowledge of cooking of various herbs associated with the preparation of different potions made her an invaluable attendant to Jonathan Quimby. Dr. Quimby learned that his pretty young assistant also had another specialty — as a midwife. He learned much from the woman who assumed the name Lydia Briar. As the result of her expertise, his own reputation advanced.

Traveling to plantations surrounding Williamsburg, he often brought along his assistant especially when the patient was a woman in the last stages of expectancy. He marveled at her extraordinary ability in such cases and was more than happy to pay her an uncommonly high wage for a woman of that era. While his own reputation as a man of medicine was on the rise, he fostered a quiet understanding with Lydia that she'd be rewarded for her not-so-well-known but nevertheless, treasured assistance. He made good on that promise.

Lydia found happiness and peace in the lovely and lively town of Williamsburg. She spent forty years there outliving Dr. Quimby. She worked for his son during the 1730's when life in Colonial Virginia reached its fullest bloom. The younger Dr. Quimby, who grew up watching Lydia assist his father, kept true to the instructions from the elder's deathbed — to provide for Lydia and retain her as an employee.

In his youth, Spencer Quimby fell in love with Lydia Briar. To his dismay, he understood that his interest was unrequited. Lydia was not concerned with any matters of the heart for she would rather spend her time helping women give birth. Though still retained as an assistant to the younger Dr. Quimby, Lydia lived in a small house to the rear of the Apothecary Shop, which she purchased from the estate of the elder Dr. Quimby a few years prior to her sixtieth birthday.

Spencer Quimby persisted in his desires for Lydia. His persistence ranged from small things, such as samples of new herbs and elixirs that he procured on his annual trips to the northern seaports, to more sharp strategies such as showing up at her door with bouquets of hollyhocks and daffodils when the seasons provided.

Gradually over a protracted period of time, this strategy produced incremental dividends. From what began as a polite thank you and to his surprise, the reward for these attentions progressed to where Lydia accompanied him on Sunday afternoon outings to the Palace Green. It stretched between the Governor's Palace to the northeast and Duke of Gloucester Street to the southwest and was lined on both sides by columns of large oak trees and stately homes.

Williamsburg in the 1720's and 1730's saw its fortunes at high tide. Colonial life was in its unmistakable prime, although most of those who lived it had no idea of how relatively calm their mere existence would prove to be. At one end of Duke of Gloucester Street adjacent to the Apothecary Shop and Lydia's home, stood the beautiful and imposing Capitol. There, the Colonial House of Burgesses were busy debating the intricacies of Indian treaties and the complex relationship they had with the Crown of England. One mile to the southwest at the end of this same street lay the equally imposing and recently completed Wren Building of the College of William and Mary, so named for its architect, Sir Christopher Wren. In this building, young men of the cloth would study for ordination. Along with them studied future giants of law and jurisprudence who would document a case for independence from the crown and then create a new nation in the ensuing decades.

From the College to the Capitol, Duke of Gloucester Street was, by far, the busiest mile in Colonial Virginia. The various shops and stalls of Merchants Square were followed by Bruton Parish Church and the Palace Green on the left side of the street. On the right, stretched a procession of every type of trade smith imaginable along with the Palace Guard's Powder Magazine. As one neared the Capitol, a series of taverns and lodgings, accompanied by handsome residences, lined the wide thoroughfare. These establishments accommodated the visiting Burgesses from all parts of the Virginia Colony when the legislature was in session.

Sunday afternoons on the Palace Green provided the happiest of times when Colonial Williamsburg was in full flower. Young couples walked along its well-grazed lawns with feminine hands on masculine arms. It provided the place and time when people of means showed their finery in clothing and carriage. Children ran alongside chasing their barrel hoops or engaged in games of hopscotch and Ring a Ring o' Roses. Older married men challenged one another to games of lawn bowling and horseshoes while wives exchanged recipes and tidbits of the latest gossip.

Chief among the hot topics of this gossip was speculation about the town's apothecary and his frequent companion; the vexing blonde midwife assistant whose background was much mysteried. Such whispers did not go unnoticed by Lydia who, while growing warmer towards the affections of her younger would-be suitor, nevertheless became less comfortable on their Sunday afternoon outings.

In part, fueled by the scorn for such interclass courtship (the idea of a prominent apothecary lavishing his attentions on his assistant, a midwife), the gossip was further heated by an incendiary mixture of jealousy for Lydia's beauty and the desire of these matrons to match their own daughters with such a handsome, successful and eligible bachelor. Lydia's only defense was her ever increasing reputation as one of the most competent midwives in the entire Virginia colony.

The Broom

Her skills in this arena — with particular proficiency in the management of complicated and unusually difficult deliveries — caught the attention and the gratitude of highly placed families on both shores of the James River. In time, her reputation would spread from prosperous Norfolk at the river's mouth all the way to the river's falls, which rushed alongside the fledgling village named for the Earl of Richmond.

Like her or not, the women of Williamsburg tampered their disdain for Lydia in light of the great value she brought when she was needed most. Time and time again, Lydia was there when a woman faced her worst predicament. It was simply uncanny how Lydia arrived upon the scene, at just the right moment with or without a summons for assistance. Even though such fortuitous arrivals had the potential for supernatural speculation as to possible connections to the occult, the end result was simple — lives, infantile and maternal were saved by Lydia again and again and again.

Chapter 24

By the spring of 1728, the courtship of Spencer Quimby and Lydia Briar invited inquiry into whether or not the two would ever marry. Spencer, himself, got a loud and clear message from the town-folk to press the issue of matrimony. Repeatedly, he engaged in conversation with Lydia all designed to arrive upon the moment of proposal. Yet Lydia, cognizant of her own true background and the many years that in truth separated them, always managed to change the subject. Finally frustrated with his own repeated failure to ask the ultimate question, he blurted it out one day upon her answering a knock at the door.

"Lydia," he popped, "will you marry me?"

"Come in Spencer," she replied. "I don't care who sees you, come in."

As delicately as she was able, she declined his offer and fashioned a ruse that he had to accept. She said that she lost her virginity as a teenage girl when she was raped by an Indian. She went on to say that the rape resulted in pregnancy that led to complications which caused a stillborn child. Now she suffered a barren womb. Lydia knew that Spencer's family would press him for an heir to their vast landholdings and that Spencer would want a son to come into the apothecary practice. She then said that her 'barrenness' did not proscribe sexual union, a not-too-subtle hint that he might have his way with her if that was his desire.

This disclosure was how a young apothecary began a steamy affair with his youthful-appearing midwife assistant. Their rendezvous were frequent but, given the staid and stoic standards of their times, discretion was the overriding all-encompassing concern to Lydia and Spencer. Their risky liaisons were overflowing with all of the passions that could be bound within the britches and corsets that clothed the lovers of that day. The mere fact of the discretionary demands mandated by their times only served to intensify the heat that stoked the coals of their desire.

Despite the intensity of their lovemaking however, they both realized the substantial risks involved in the pursuit of private pleasure. First, there were all of the societal dangers of getting caught in the act, and if not, discovered in the fact. After all, fornication was not merely deemed to be immoral but illegal as well.

Laws against consensual sex between unwed adults were ponderous indeed. A man caught in such situations could well face the pillory or the lash or both. Any woman caught whoring about was permanently branded on the cheek with the letter — **A** — for adulteress. She might also face the prospect of prison or being summarily banished from the community.

Even aside from the punitive legal consequences were the risks associated with the societal ramifications of being discovered. Although Spencer Quimby had something of an exclusivity for his much-needed business, patronage of that business would be severely impacted if its proprietor were found to be engaged in dalliance. While the gentlemen of Williamsburg might easily find humor and perhaps admiration in the activity of a young man-about-town, their wives would surely temper such latent approval with scornful contempt and condemnation. Invitations to all but a very few social gatherings so necessary to the facilitation of commerce would cease being extended and Spencer Quimby might well find himself banished from the Bruton Parish Church.

As for Lydia, being branded an adulteress or even suspected of being a whore, would mean the end of her considerable career as Spencer's midwife assistant. That much was a certainty despite her renowned skill and competence. Nothing short of being run out of town was a decidedly real consequence of having her liaisons with Spencer Quimby come to the forefront.

Despite all these very real and hazardous risks, the affair continued for some time. It is a testament to the high degree of intelligence on both their parts that the carnal nature of their relationship could never be substantiated beyond rumor. Not that there was any lack of effort on the parts of envious and nosy people to inquire, to spy and to pry into just what was going on between these two.

Any hint of impropriety and every nuance of indication was thoroughly examined and followed, but always to no avail. The fact of the matter was that Spencer and Lydia were able to outwit and elude the prying eyes of suspicion and subsequently maintain the appearance of mere companionship for its own sake. This of course only served to fan the flames of suspicion all the more.

Chapter 25

In order to thwart the ever-growing suspicions surrounding all of the speculation as to the more salacious aspects of their friendship, Lydia and Spencer agreed to limit the number of visits she made to the Apothecary Shop. After all, the colonial Capitol of Virginia loomed less than a few hundred yards east of Spencer's practice.

By the precisely same amount of distance to the north stood the Public Gaol (jail) where prisoners awaiting trial were locked away for safekeeping. Such close proximity to the two bastions of colonial justice, those being trial and punishment, had not escaped the minds of Spencer Quimby and Lydia Briar.

Also situated between the apothecary shop and the Public Gaol, just happened to be the house that Lydia had purchased from the estate of Spencer's father, Jonathan Quimby. Therefore, Spencer was not able to call on Lydia at her residence. In fact, he never knocked at the door nor entered her house following that first passionate encounter at the onset of their affair.

It certainly was not proper for Lydia to knock at Spencer's door either. Part of the problem was that his Williamsburg residence, a modest home located one block south of the Apothecary Shop on Francis Street was in a heavily traveled area. Built next door to the town's master gunsmith's shop, few of the patrons would have missed seeing the comings and goings of such an attractive woman. Further inhibiting such visits were the contemporary standards of a society where ladies simply did not knock at the doors of young gentlemen.

One block southwest of the apothecary shop on the other side of Duke of Gloucester Street stood Tarpley's Store, a compact two-story edifice located next door to Wetherburn's Tavern. Spencer Quimby often frequented Tarpley's for various supplies. Because of a convoluted arrangement between Mr. Tarpley and the elder Dr. Quimby, which much resembled the modern concept of consignment inventory, such supplies were stored in an upstairs room and only paid for once the items left the premises. It was up to Dr. Quimby and his son later to manage the transactions themselves by leaving a record of each transaction with the clerk downstairs.

Because of the demands of the apothecary business, Spencer gave Lydia the same access to Tarpley's upstairs room that he enjoyed. Since he, Lydia and old Mr. Tarpley were the only ones allowed access to this room, it provided a conveniently discreet place for Lydia and Spencer to act on their passions.

With the exception of acting in a professional capacity, Lydia being a de facto employee of Spencer Quimby avoided being seen with Spencer (and vice versa) save for their Sunday strolls along the Palace Green. This was hardly enough to quell the busy mill of gossip surrounding their situation, but it did serve to keep such gossip in check.

As the years wore on, the passionate evenings mellowed into a more genuine friendship between the two. By the middle 1730's, what had been heated passion evolved into less physical and more congenial companionship. The two occasional lovers genuinely liked each other as mere friends, and the mere fact of sexual infrequence served the dual purpose of scandal avoidance and less complicated interaction between Dr. Spencer Quimby and his midwife assistant. In 1736, Lydia turned sixty, but this fact was kept secret to herself so that she might be able to avoid suspicion. She appeared to be a woman in her late thirties while she shrewdly claimed to be less than fifty years of age. Still quite attractive, she amazed local men and women alike, with her youthful appearance and energy.

In what spare time she had, she devoted much of it to outfitting her modest home with the finest lace curtains her savings could buy. With one room at a time, she added pieces of furniture crafted by Robert Green a local cabinet maker. In 1738, she assisted Mrs. Green with the birth of her first son, Robert, Jr., and was rewarded with a beautifully crafted bureau in lieu of payment. Grateful for such a stunning addition to her home, Lydia befriended the Greens during the next decade while she assisted them in the birth of six more children including a son, Isaac, born in 1741.

All was not so blissful however as the 1740's wore on. By the middle of the decade, people began anew to whisper about this woman who claimed to be approaching sixty and yet appeared not to be a day over forty-two. At first, it was merely envious women whose husbands' wandering eyes aroused their contempt. Then, the men whispered amongst themselves about this attractive woman who was employed by the apothecary shop for some forty years.

By the time Lydia traveled to the Tucker plantation in 1748 to assist Mrs. Tucker in the birth of her daughter, Sarah, rumblings within the social fabric of Williamsburg about Lydia Briar were brought to the official attention of Governor Dinwiddie. It was then that Governor Dinwiddie subsequently ordered an investigation into her background.

Following the birth of Sarah Tucker, Lydia returned home and was placed under house arrest pending full investigation by order of Virginia's colonial governor. With two guards posted at the door of her house, Lydia had no choice but to invoke her old powers and flee. Opening an upstairs dormer, she sat upon her broom and was gone before anyone discovered her escape.

Chapter 26

To be entirely accurate, Lydia lived in Williamsburg precisely forty-six years. During that time, she watched it grow into a thriving town, which boasted newspapers, schools of higher education and theatrical offerings that rivaled any in the Western Hemisphere. The seeds of independence were sowed in the debates that took place in its House of Burgesses. Although the year of 1748 saw almost universal loyalty towards the British Crown, the slow move towards revolution began, albeit unwittingly, in the discourse of political debate. As if it was so very gradual to be intentionally camouflaged, Virginia's continued dependence on the crown began its fateful demise.

The extended metamorphosis of thought was temporarily assuaged when the French decided to build two forts on the Ohio River five years after Lydia took her leave of Williamsburg. Governor Dinwiddie dispatched a dashing, young militia officer to voice his formal protests against such intrusions. After entertaining the young officer with fine wine, stewed pheasant and a welcoming reception, the French informed the major that it was he who was trespassing on French soil — his name — George Washington. The next year saw his return leading a force of militiamen and his unit experienced initial success at repelling the French forces. Unfortunately however, later that same year witnessed his surrender on July 4, 1754, and this gave effective control of the entire region to France.

While these French and Indian Wars were fought, Lydia slowly moved toward the high country of western Virginia. In the course of her westward sojourn, Lydia stopped at a number of plantations along the James River, giving aid and comfort to women in parturition. She decided that her next home should be located away from others and set high among the blue slopes at the edge of Virginia's vast frontier. At the ideal spot, she found a bluff overlooking the Rockfish River in the northern tip of Nelson County. It was there that she built her one-room cabin.

During the house's construction (it was essentially completed by her eightieth birthday), Lydia found that flying on her broomstick offered several advantages. First, it enabled her to travel to and from the courthouse markets in Charlottesville to procure supplies necessary for the construction of a home. Her visits to these markets provided much merriment to Albemarle County locals who wondered where and how a woman, well along into her *fifties*, could build her own house. Repeated inquiries brought nothing in reply from the aging woman and yet her reputation as a competent midwife made Lydia a valued member of the community.

Secondly, the ability to cover considerable distances in relatively short periods of time ensured that her house would not be found by curious acquaintances. She lost some of the energy required for long walks, so brooming enabled her to move around quickly and efficiently. Lastly, it made traveling to women who needed her assistance all the easier. She reduced these trips focusing instead on the more recent settlements situated along the banks of the Rockfish River. She already used some of the money given to her by grateful husbands to purchase cornmeal and flour from Josiah Wood. As a young militiaman who fought alongside Major Washington in 1755, he established a gristmill near the Rockfish two years later, on land ceded to him by the House of Burgesses, for gallantry in action. Breveted to the rank of lieutenant by Washington himself, Lieutenant Wood was equally adept in matters of business. He took a liking to this shrewd old woman, who ably bargained for extra measures of grain and who lived somewhere up in the hills overlooking Wood's Mill.

When Lieutenant Wood took a wife, it became apparent that the couple would establish one of the leading families in Nelson County. Lydia Thorn (she was again using her real name) was there to assist Mrs. Wood with the birth of her children. She also struck up a friendship with Spoons, the butler, and enjoyed visiting with him when the opportunity presented itself.

Of course, there were sides to Lydia that she concealed. Although witchcraft hysteria largely subsided in recent decades, she nevertheless took great care not to broom where she might be seen. She was never sure that inquisitions might not return. She was wise not to display her powers. Aside from brooming, Lydia rarely used her other witchcraft-enabled skills. Afraid that Tituba might somehow sense her whereabouts by detecting such magic was a fear Lydia dreaded most.

She lived quietly in her modest one-room house overlooking the Rockfish River. She spent much of her time witnessing the steady stream of settlement along its banks. Contented by the idea that she kept her home unfettered and without interruption, Lydia Thorn watched the seasons change. Autumnal brilliance gave way to winter snows and stillness. The rush of the river swelled by the melting snow quenched the trees and blossoms of spring as life renewed. The warmth of summer elicited nature in her full force with trees and animals and men and mountains all inexorably linked in much activity.

Lydia kept a low fire burning in her stone hearth that she, herself, built. Sitting in her rocker one warm summer's day, Lydia was just about to add another log to a dwindling glow when, in the very week of her ninetieth birthday, a knock arrived upon her door.

Who could it possibly be, and why were they here? How did they find their way to her house, as it was so high up on the slope of the ancient mountain? Lydia said nothing. A second knock. Lydia then invoked one of her powers and vanished into a puff of smoke. The door opened. It was Isaac Green who stood there nearly exhausted and desperately seeking help for his pregnant wife, Sarah Tucker Green.

Chapter 27

After returning from maneuvers, Nathan Green was visited by the old woman. On that fateful night, she related the story of his birth and then left. At first, Nathan was stunned by all she revealed. Subsequent visits from the old woman proved to be even more astonishing. Lydia, after swearing him to absolute secrecy, told him her past. Now living in her one hundred and fifteenth year, she was completely reliant upon her broom to get around. It was very obvious to Nathan she was old, but if what she was saying was true (and he was beginning to believe it for himself), then she was indeed one hundred fifteen years old.

He remained silent about these revelations when visiting his fiancée, as he did not wish to make her pre-marital jitters worse nor did he wish to upset her father who might then withdraw his consent.

Lydia carried the broom with her when she arrived at his door. And, she always arrived after sunset. The fact of her advanced age and the absence of any dwellings within a few miles led Nathan to conclude that she must have the ability to fly about on a broomstick.

The revelation that Lydia attended to the birth of Anne Wood was easy to accept. Rumors of an elderly midwife, who arrived at the moment children were born, were part of the local folklore of the Rockfish River. When she subsequently informed him she was also there for the birth of his parents, Nathan was understandably astonished. Her knowledge of his grandparents, from what little he was able to learn from his own father, proved that she must have known both the Tuckers and the Greens. He learned that his father was apprenticed as a carpenter and that his grandfather was a cabinetmaker who crafted some of the finest furniture in Williamsburg.

He learned much from the old woman about his mother's family too. Sarah Tucker was born into a large and prosperous family who operated a large plantation on the James River. Her father, who emigrated from England in the late 1720's as an indentured servant, rose from the humble circumstances of his arrival to establish one of the finest plantations in Virginia. Not one to forget about his former station in life, John Tucker raised all of his children to prepare them for manual labor in the event fortunes would take a turn for the worse. While they were schooled in the arts of cooking, dancing and sewing, his daughters were also expected to work in the gardens, so they would never know hunger. This was precisely how Nathan's parents were able to survive that first harsh winter in Nelson County.

Nathan learned that, although she was determined to help her husband scratch out a living in the wilderness, Sarah was painfully thin and frail. This contributed to her death while giving birth to her only child. Lydia went on to say that his father was so saddened by the loss of his wife that he was truly a changed man following her death.

In early December, Nathan worked up the courage to ask Lydia what prompted her to tell him everything. After all, here was this woman who witnessed tremendous change throughout her life and who was forced to stay on the run. She was there when England established a colonial foothold in North America and lived to witness the birth of a new nation.

She coughed and then paused as if considering her words. "I lived my life in a way that was not of my own choosing. The only man I loved and from whom you received your given name, Nathan, was taken from me by his father. The only child I ever had was given up so that he could have a chance at a better life. The only child I ever loved, though not my own, was brutally murdered by the one person who was responsible for all the unpleasantness that followed me. I have lived long Nathan, but I have not lived well.

"All my years are catching up with me. My health …" she coughed "… is starting to wane. I feel it necessary to tell someone my story. Much has been locked away in my heart for longer than I can remember. My memories will soon fail me and then I will have nothing except this old broom. A broom which has been with me since I left London so many years ago." Lydia coughed again.

Nathan wanted to know what made her decide to tell him.

"I have watched you grow from an infant without a mother to love. You are a fine young man. I have seen you as a child wanting a closeness with your father that was denied to you because of his grief. I witnessed the true devotion you have toward your intended. I know what is in your heart is pure. I will be there for the birth of your children …" Lydia laughed, "… if I don't die beforehand."

Nathan smiled.

"I need you to do something for me, Nathan."

"What is it you need?"

Coughing again, she replied, "There is a tiny house high on the mountain." She pointed to the southwest. "You will receive a sign when I leave this world. When you do, go up into that mountain and find my home. I will have placed my feet into the fire. Take the ashes that remain and go to the top of the mountain. Scatter me to the wind so I may rest. If you do not do exactly as I ask, I cannot escape the curse of hell that otherwise awaits me."

Nathan shook his head. "Yes I will."

The door opened and Lydia sat upon her broom and was gone.

Nathan stood stunned by the sight of this elderly woman flying away on her broom. His mouth opened wide as Lydia disappeared into the night sky. He closed his door and walked across the room to the hearth. Poking at the coals, he added a log before sitting down.

The solitude to which he had grown accustomed in the years following his father's death thus enabled Nathan to deeply ponder life's great mysteries. The extraordinary array of circumstances regarding Lydia Thorn required introspective reflection to a far greater degree than that which was more typically warranted.

Nathan sat alone, staring into the flames that so often captured the essence of his thoughts. Within the fire's playful dance emerged the realization that destiny played a hand in the intermingling of so many lives. The strange turn of fate with intricately woven sequences, conspired to bring Nathan to this place, seemed to hinge on events tied to the life of this one very old woman. Ironically, her destiny was dependent upon the actions of a man, whose very existence was owed to her in ways that transcended geography and generation. Even though he was cognizant of the importance that this woman had tied to her final request, Nathan felt humbled by the enormity of what lay in the balance. Failure to carry out her wishes precisely as she had instructed would condemn her soul to hell. There was simply no way he could fail her. Of this, he was certain.

He thought about the sign. The fear that he might overlook such a sign in the course of more temporal distractions frightened Nathan. After all, he might walk right past it or not recognize the significance of it. Such a lack of awareness could doom her chances of deliverance. He wished that she were more specific when she spoke of this sign.

In the three weeks that existed between the night of her last visit and his wedding, he thought about the old woman's sign and all it represented. These thoughts did nothing to accelerate the slowness with which the days seemed to pass. In spite of the fact that the sun's slow progression to the south shortened the daylight hours of December, the days became ever longer for Nathan Green. In the frost-hardened ground of Greenfield Farm, the stillness of the oncoming winter sought to dampen the progress of the minutes and hours that constitute the brevity of a lifetime.

Chapter 28

Nathan completed his morning chores. The cows were fed with hay that was cut and stacked the previous summer. A section of his field was seeded with winter rye in an effort to replenish the rich nutrients robbed by corn in previous months. He saddled his horse, which he purchased in Schuyler, and noticed that the sun now topped the early winter sky. He returned to the house as it came time to change his attire.

The only suit of clothes he owned that was appropriate for formal occasions was his militia uniform. With only the spacing of brass buttons to indicate his rank, Sergeant Green donned his regimental attire. He studied his reflection in the mirror that topped his mother's bureau and drifted in the image it beheld.

Then he looked about the large room to assure himself that the premises were sufficiently neat and tidy. Satisfied that the house was worthy to receive his bride, he walked onto the porch closing the door behind. He stared for a minute at the rolling waters of the Rockfish River. The elm tree, under which his parents rested, had already dropped its brown leaves. Neither Isaac nor Sarah would be there to witness the marriage of their son. Nathan's eyes welled with tears. He walked across the yard to the tree.

"Father … today I am to be married to the daughter of a man you know. Although you never got on well with Lieutenant Wood, I believe you would come to love his daughter as if she were your own. I tried to take good care of the farm. Now I will have someone to share my life with.

"Mother … I never got a chance to know you. Father told me very little. I learned much from the midwife. She knew both of your families. I think of you when I read your Bible. I wish you could have met the woman I'm going to marry. I think you would love her. I hope you won't mind her wearing your ring."

Nathan was sobbing now. He wiped his eyes with a white linen handkerchief and blew his nose. Returning the handkerchief to his pocket, he turned and walked slowly to his horse. With one brief glance toward the house his parents built, Nathan mounted his steed and was off to Wood's Mill.

The ride along the trail by the river gave Nathan an opportunity to think about his fiancée. The air was crisp on this Christmas Eve and returned the color to his face. The woods along the riverbank were quiet and the rolling river glistened brightly in the light of a brilliant sun. Nathan glanced up and was impressed with the deep blue sky that, on this day, knew no cloud.

What a glorious day to be wed, he thought as he continued his journey toward a bride and a new life.

By the time Nathan rode into Wood's Mill, many guests from the neighboring counties of Albemarle and Nelson had arrived. Prominent citizens from as far away as Charlottesville and Lovingston made the journey on this Christmas eve to see the daughter of Lieutenant Josiah Wood marry one of his militiamen.

Among those present at the wedding was James Monroe of Ash Lawn-Highland (later to be known as simply Ash Lawn). He was elected to the Senate that year in spite of his fervent opposition to Constitutional ratification. Also present was his ally, Thomas Jefferson of Monticello who returned from France to serve as Washington's

Secretary of State. Widowed nine years before, Jefferson was accompanied by his daughter, Patsy. The president, who was unable to attend, sent along a beautiful set of silver toasting goblets and a note expressing his heartfelt congratulations.

Such an impressive guest list might intimidate a groom of Sergeant Green's stature, but Nathan realized these great men were here because of the high esteem in which they held for Anne's father. As he entered the house, he was shown to the parlor by Spoons where he met Reverend Yancey. It was only then that many of the guests discovered that this common soldier was the bridegroom. As he stood, Anne nervously waited upstairs.

At a few minutes past two o'clock, the procession began with Anne's mother leading the way. Following her three sisters dressed in green, Anne entered the room on the arm of her father. The bride, resplendent in the satin and lace gown that accentuated her shapely form, held a festive bouquet of holly and mistletoe. Her full bosom was perfectly suited to the dress with her cleavage yet visible through the screen of her veil. Indeed, Nathan was not alone in his awe of this beautiful young lady.

When Lieutenant Wood announced that he so "giveth of this woman to be the bride," he took his seat beside her mother while the young couple wed. Essentially, the ceremony lasted but a few minutes, although it did seem longer to the bride and her groom. After Reverend Yancey blessed the couple in the Name of the Father and of the Son and of the Holy Ghost, Nathan peeled back the veil and kissed his new wife. The only problem was that he did so before the preacher had pronounced them man and wife and this fell much to the amusement of everyone in the room including the bride's parents. Not as amused however was Reverend Yancey who briefly frowned in disapproval at the upstart groom. Nevertheless, he finished the ritual and smiled at the embarrassed couple when it became duly official. Nathan escorted Anne Wood Green from the room to the congratulatory applause of the many guests assembled. He was followed by the bridesmaids, Lieutenant and

Mrs. Wood and the Reverend Yancey. The eight principal players formed a reception line in the stately hall.

The procession of visitors was slow moving. Nathan did not recall having met so many people in a single place and time in his entire life. Some of the guests were officers in the militia and Nathan knew many of them. He had never before met Mr. Jefferson nor Mr. Monroe who lived not far from Nathan's farm, despite having heard much about these two brilliant individuals prior to this day.

Anne, on the other hand, knew practically everyone. She grew up in the company of these people and every one of them complimented her dress or how beautiful a woman she had become. She was gracious in her acknowledgment of such flattery smiling warmly but still managing to maintain a reserved sense of dignity. She was absolutely radiant on this afternoon. Her classically shaped jaw joined to form a delicately perfect chin and supported her beaming smile in a way that made her universally desirable. Her ivory skin was positively without flaw and her fiery blue eyes glistened in the afternoon sun that peeked through the windowpanes.

When the last of the guests greeted the wedding party and were shown into the dining room, they were followed by the bride and groom. The cook, at the direction of Mrs. Wood, prepared a sumptuous Christmas feast. Roast venison, smoked ham and a Christmas pie of various wild fowl baked in an elliptical pastry coffin were set on the lengthy tables that were joined together. Complimented with boiled onions, glazed lady apples, turnips, carrots and a wine jelly mold, the table offered a wide array of breads.

On the various sideboards were the delectable desserts including sweet potato pie, bourbon pecan cake, sour cherry trifle and marzipan. The centerpiece was a large plum pudding that seductively towered above the sweet temptations. Madeira wine was served along with syllabub. The eggnog proved to be the talk of the table. Many of the guests were introduced to that delectable drink for the first time.

Following dinner, an outpouring of toasts honoring the couple spewed forth from the men seated alongside their wives. Of notable eloquence was the raised glass offered by Mr. Jefferson whose prosaic dedication brought tears from both Mrs. Wood and her husband.

"To Mr. and Mrs. Nathan Green," Mr. Jefferson said. "May the rich soil of your fields yield a bounteous crop. May the winding path of life's journey be absent of peril and pestilence. May the love you share this Christmas Eve flare eternal in times of wind and storm. Long life and happiness to both of you always."

After Lieutenant Wood offered his salutation to his daughter and son-in-law, Nathan rose and held up his glass. He looked around at the gathering and proudly said, "I would wish to express my appreciation to all who have come to share in this ceremony. I also wish to thank Lieutenant Wood and Mrs. Wood (looking over at the woman), or I should say Mother, for the way they have accepted me into their family and for the lovely feast we enjoyed this afternoon. However, I can only offer one toast tonight and that is to my bride."

With that, everyone at the table stood and raised their glasses to Anne whose eyes welled with tears. She tried to speak but her words failed. She could only offer a gentle smile while the others chimed in unison.

"Here, here!"

Sipping on sweet Madeira, they sat and awaited the serving of many desserts.

Nathan and Anne, though surrounded by her relatives and guests, felt as if they were alone. Looking into her eyes, Nathan kissed Anne as if they were, in fact, by themselves.

Mr. Monroe chimed in. "There will be plenty of time for that later, now won't there?"

The laughter following this commentary was considerable.

Nathan blushed as did Anne while Lieutenant Wood frowned and loudly cleared his throat. Then he too smiled at his friend shaking his head. Before the afternoon's festivities were complete, the guests were favored with a rare and special treat courtesy of Spoons the butler. He sat in a chair at the far end of the table opposite Anne and Nathan. In being the house servant that he was, this was more than enough in and of itself to quiet the guests and arouse their undivided attention. He held two spoons, back to back in his right hand while holding his left hand above the spoons. He struck the spoons in rhythmic fashion against his knee. Sometimes strumming the spoons along his fingers, he amazed his audience with the musical skill from which his name derived.

After a while, he stopped and looked over at Anne. He smiled broadly. The guests erupted into a burst of applause. With that, Spoons stood, bowed twice and left.

The time had come for Nathan and Anne to leave Wood's Mill. She kissed her parents on the cheek mingling her tears with theirs. Nathan kissed Mrs. Wood and shook the lieutenant's hand. Exiting the front door, Nathan was surprised to find that a military honor guard waited for them on each side of the stairs leading down from the porch.

"Atten-*tion!*" snapped Lieutenant Wood.

The soldiers obeyed.

"Present *arms!*"

The soldiers raised their muskets in their right hand while saluting at waist level with their left. A drummer played a drum roll while the couple descended the staircase. When Nathan and Anne stepped on the ground, the drum roll stopped.

"Order arms!" Lieutenant Wood commanded.

Nathan and Mrs. Wood watched as the newlyweds climbed into Wood's carriage that was hitched to Nathan's horse. The Greens were escorted by the detachment of militia back to Greenfield on the orders of Lieutenant Wood.

Nathan was surprised that such honors was bestowed upon a non-commissioned officer. However, there was an ulterior motive in the mind of his father-in-law. Since it was getting dark, the lieutenant thought it best to have an armed escort accompany the couple to their home, so he had the foresight to make such arrangements in advance.

The carriage was driven by one of the soldiers who returned it, hitched to another horse, to Wood's Mill later that night. The remaining soldiers marched alongside the carriage with two bearing torches in front to light the way. During the five-mile journey, Anne and Nathan said little to each other as they rode to the place that would be their home. They were exhausted from the day's events and felt somewhat awkward being escorted in such a manner.

When at last they arrived at Greenfield, Nathan was surprised to find two sentries posted at his front door. When the couple climbed the staircase, the sentries came to attention. Nathan asked why they had been so posted. The sentries declined to answer and instead opened the door to reveal that a blazing fire was roaring in the fireplace.

Lieutenant Wood thought of everything.

One of the sentries said, "By your leave, Sergeant, we shall now return to Wood's Mill. Is there anything else the sergeant might require?"

"No thank you, and a Merry Christmas to you and your men," Nathan replied.

"Merry Christmas to you Sergeant and you, ma'am."

The soldiers then walked down the steps and joined the others for the return to Wood's Mill. Here at last, the newlywed couple found themselves alone. A bottle of Madeira and two stem glasses were set upon the table.

"Father thought of everything," Anne said.

"He most certainly did darling." Nathan removed his uniform coat and saber. He looked at his wife. Her face was aglow in the light of the fire that had warmed the room. Never was she so beautiful and so appealing. She smiled and stepped closer. She removed her veil, pulled a hairpin and her light brown locks fell upon her shoulders. They kissed passionately, more passionately than ever before.

"You're going to have to help me out of this, love," she said referring to her wedding gown. He trembled. She turned and stood with her back to him. "Please help me with these buttons."

His hands shook as he struggled to unlatch the tiny maze that was located between her shoulders. He undid the other buttons situated in the small of her back, and she slipped out of the gown. In doing so, the laces of her corset were revealed. Nathan stood motionless.

"Could you please untie me?"

He said nothing.

She separated the sides of her corset and set it on the table. She gathered her wedding gown and placed it over the back of the chair. Turning toward her husband wearing only her undergarments, she smiled. He looked at her, his mouth slightly ajar and he sensed that she might be able to hear the pounding of his heart. After fumbling with the buttons, he removed his waistcoat while using his feet to remove his boots.

He could see that her nipples stood erect beneath her under-blouse. She crossed her arms over her breasts seemingly to hide them and blushed. With her arms still crossed, she placed her hands on the shoulders of her chemise and pulled along her upper arms. Her chest was heaving as the chemise was lowered along the rising slope of her full breasts. Nathan inhaled sharply. He took Anne into his arms and carried her to the bed that awaited them. In the glow of the fire, Nathan and Anne released their pent-up passions and consummated their marriage on that Christmas 'eve in 1790.

Chapter 29

Their lovemaking continued throughout the night as the passionate flames that burned within them outlasted the fire from the hearth. Nathan could not imagine the pleasures with which Anne bestowed onto him. Again and again during the course of their first night, he *feasted* upon the rich and tempting body of his wife.

The first time he entered her was difficult for Anne, but he was a patient lover and managed to arouse her natural desires. After five heated encounters, her moaning became vocal and the two collapsed in an ocean of climactic wailing. It was after this sixth time that Nathan and Anne fell into a deep slumber. By then, the fire was reduced to a crimson glow. So exhausted were they that their bodies were still joined when they fell asleep.

The following morning, they woke naked and shivering. The fire was out. Anne sat up in bed covering her breasts with the blankets that were haphazardly strewn about. She looked out of the window. The snow covered the ground and was still falling. Nathan reached for a blanket and wrapped it around his shoulders. He kissed his wife.

"I've got to get a fire going." His teeth chattered.

Nathan went to work on the hearth. When he knew the fire would last, he returned to his shivering wife and embraced her. She lay on top of him and the couple continued to shake in the coldness of the room. Covered with every blanket and comforter they owned he felt her breasts pressing against his chest. He sensed every detail of her body as though his body was painstakingly scanning her own. He loved the way her breasts pressed against his upper abdomen and her pubic hair on his right leg.

Anne felt her husband becoming erect and before long he was once again inside her. As they made love for the seventh time, the snow fell that Christmas morning. Greenfield was as white as the dress she had worn the day before.

Chapter 30

High atop Devil's Knob, Lydia Thorn braced herself for yet another winter. During the course of her life, the seasons came full circle one hundred and fifteen times. Now, although her eyes were too weak to see the life that teemed at the foot of the mountain, she sensed she would be making one more journey to Greenfield Farm in about ten months-time. She spent this Christmas, as she had spent so many Christmases, alone. Rising only to add an occasional log to the small fire that burned in her fireplace, or to give the bubbling cauldron an intermittent stir, Lydia reflected on her life while the snow drifted around her hovel.

She thought about the child she bore and left on the doorstep of a Pennsylvania woodsman and wondered what had become of him. She pondered as to whether he grew as young Sean McComas might have grown had he not been brutally murdered that one horrible night. She heard nothing of the wretched Tituba since then and was able to take some solace in the fact that she escaped her evil grasp.

Nathan Parris, with all of those she had known in Salem, was surely gone from this world. She felt she could have married Spencer Quimby but probably spared him grief by avoiding his persistent proposals. Unless he grew to be quite old himself, he probably passed on as well.

As the wind outside howled up the eastern slope, December turned into January. The drifting snow piled alongside her home even though brief respites of sunlight alternated the series of storms arising from the southeast. January gave way to February and the snow kept coming and coming. Lydia rocked away the time in her chair with her feet propped upon a stool before the warmth of the fire.

By the middle of March, the wind was stronger. The air, nevertheless, warmed as evidenced by the sound of water dripping from the melting snow. The water gained momentum as it rushed down the side of the mountain finding small streams to flow toward larger ones. Ultimately, this water found its way to the Rockfish River that ran along the banks of both Greenfield Farm and Wood's Mill.

The river brought new life to the valley. After a long winter's slumber, man and beast finally stirred from their collective sanctuary and once again ventured forth into the outside world. The stillness of winter surrendered to the acceleration of spring and the air was filled with the sounds of life's renewal. On the wing and the hoof and on the fin and the foot, the world below the mountain was once again moving. High above Lydia's roof, soared an eagle who watched, circled and waited. She could hear his screeching. Spring had arrived at long last.

Chapter 31

Nathan Green could finally turn the soil of his subsistence on a March day in 1791. While he lashed the plow to his mules, his wife lay in bed. She awakened feeling sick to the stomach and had spit up into the chamber pot that very morning. It was the second time in as many days and her usually regular menstrual cycle was late.

As the sun rose into the late winter's sky, Nathan heard the screeching of an eagle as it circled atop the mountain that overlooked his farm. He tilled the rows of his fields preparing them for the planting of peas and corn that would take place in a few weeks.

He wondered if his wife was correct in her self-diagnosis. If she were indeed correct, there would be yet another mouth to feed within the year. The prospect of having a son or daughter was at once exciting and yet frightening. He glanced over at the elm where his parents lay buried and halted the mules.

"If Anne's right, your grandchild will be born this year. God willing," he said aloud. "I just wish that both of you could be here when the time comes."

Nathan returned his attention to the mules and striking the reins on their backs yelled, "Yah!" He resumed his plowing and his mind drifted.

He wondered about whether or not Lydia Thorn would be there to help his wife when the time came.

She always had a knack for showing up before, he said to himself. *I expect she'll know when to be here provided she's still alive.*

Frequently, he wondered how an elderly woman could survive living up so high and alone. On more than one occasion, he was tempted to climb Devil's Knob and check on her. Then he thought better of it. After all, she was not the type of woman to welcome visitors.

When the sun was directly overhead, Nathan heard a loud clanging from his front porch. Glancing over, he smiled when he saw his wife holding a ladle in one hand and a saucepan in the other.

"Nathan," she hollered, "come and eat, now." His noonday meal was ready.

"Be there in a bit honey," he yelled back.

Leaving the plow where it stood, he unleashed the mules and led them down to the river. After a few minutes, he tied the pair to a tree. He walked up the hill to his house.

"Smells awfully tempting," he said walking inside. "Feeling better?"

"Much, thank you." Anne spooned some stew into a bowl and placed it before her husband. He put his arm around her and teased.

"The vittles smell tempting, too." he said laughing.

"Oh Nathan! … If you *ever* start thinking about something other than —"

"Other than what?" He leaned back, crossed his arm and winked.

"You know what," Scolding him, she blushed.

"It's mighty difficult for a man to think about something else when he's got a wife as pretty as you." He pulled her in close and kissed her.

Finally, she pushed him away. "Mr. Green you have fields to plow. And tomorrow we're going to Mother's for dinner. Reverend Yancey is coming for Sunday service. We've got to start out just after breakfast."

"I suppose I'll have to wait …" He stopped himself short. "Aw, who can wait for someone this good?" He picked up his wife in his arms and carried her to the bed. She playfully kicked her feet.

"Husband, what am I going to do with you?" She giggled.

"I expect I have a few ideas on that subject, woman." Nathan sat her on the bed.

"I expect that you do." She lifted her skirts as though it had almost become routine. "Are you ever going to get tired of this?"

"Not while there's breath in my body," he answered pulling down his breeches. "No ma-am."

Outside along the banks of the Rockfish River, a pair of mules were having an extended noonday break while their master was attending to some pressing business within his own house. For master and for mule, it would be a nice break from the rigors of farm work.

Chapter 32

It was all of two o'clock in the afternoon before Nathan had resumed his plowing. By the time he returned to the house, the sun had already set behind the ridge of mountains, and the sky was almost dark. Inside, Anne set cornbread onto the table and was serving the last of the stew she had intended for their dinner.

The air, cool and crisp, was sweetened with the fresh aroma of spring's onset. Nathan climbed the stairs, stomped his feet on the floorboards of the porch and stepped inside. He briefed Anne on the mundane details of his progress. She feigned an interest in what he was saying, partially because she felt that this was her home too. She wanted her husband to believe that his work meant as much to her as it did to him. However, her true interests were confined to those things inside the house; cooking, sewing and making a nice home for both of them.

She was extremely happy in the role of being Mrs. Nathan Green and in the probability of eventually raising a family. Yet, she also missed the hubbub of activity to which she had grown accustomed being raised at Wood's Mill.

The following morning, Nathan hitched the two-wheeled chaise to his horse. It was a crude conveyance, one which he himself built from two wheels given to him by Anne's father. He managed to rig a protective cover that adequately served the purpose of providing a safe means of transportation for his wife. Although it wasn't pretty, it was vastly superior to having her share a saddle. After Nathan rigged the chaise, he returned and breakfasted on the remaining cornbread. His wife was once again feeling nauseous and declined to partake. Nathan ate alone while Anne finished dressing.

The five-mile journey to Wood's Mill was a pleasant one. There was a slight chill to the air, and Anne kept herself warm by having her hands and feet wrapped in the wool blankets. A scarf, which hid her mouth and chin, wrapped around her neck beneath another, which she tied around her head. Only her eyes and nose were exposed to the elements. During the trip, she lowered the scarf when it started to bother her.

The sky contained only a few puffy clouds and the river glistened in the brilliant sun. Proceeding in the southerly direction as the river, the two were serenaded by the percussion of the horse's hooves, the squeaking of the wheels and the sound of the water strumming the frets of the riverbed. A melody that provided a perfect counterbalance to the woodwind harmony of robins, cardinals, orioles and blue jays. No man could compose so sweet a symphony as the yearly onset of a Virginia spring.

When they rounded the bend and approached the home of Lieutenant Wood, they noticed that the Reverend Yancey was dismounting. By the time Nathan pulled in front of the stately house, the minister had already entered through the front door. The lieutenant was the first to descend the stairs and welcome his daughter and her new husband. Mrs. Wood strode out onto the porch and greeted the couple with a beaming smile. Nathan tied his horse and followed his wife who was now on her father's arm.

The service took place in the very same room where three months before the couple were married. Reverend Yancey, not having a church of his own, traveled a circuit within the surrounding counties and ministered to their families on a rotating basis. It would be another three months before he returned to Wood's Mill. Therefore, this was a special

Sunday indeed for the Woods. Following the intimate service, they sat to a splendid meal of smoked ham, complete with a full array of complementary dishes.

The service began with readings from the New Testament followed by the hundredth Psalm, a favorite of Mrs. Wood. The sermon was about the journey of Jesus into Jerusalem. The lesson, of course, was relevant to the fact that this day was Palm Sunday. At the conclusion of his sermon, Reverend Yancey led the family in the singing of Amazing Grace. It was around noon when they all sat down to eat.

Following the meal, the Reverend announced he would have to leave, to attend to a baptism at a nearby farm. Lieutenant Wood shook his hand discreetly pressing a dollar coin into it. After seeing the reverend out, he returned to the table. Anne and her mother, who were quietly conversing during the reverend's exit, giggled. Tears flowed from their eyes. Lieutenant Wood cleared his throat and inquired as to the source of this strange behavior.

"Our Anne," said Mrs. Wood, "is with child, my husband."

Lieutenant Wood's mouth dropped. Nathan's face reddened and his eyes fell to his hands. Everyone at the table erupted into disjointed conversation. Lieutenant Wood stood, walked around to his daughter and embraced her. Then he went to Nathan, shook his hand and congratulated him.

During such times, it was natural for discussions to meander toward the subject of family and heredity. Nathan, who knew nothing of the Lieutenant's family background, was surprised to learn that Anne's father was the son of a man whose real parents were not known. Nathan was, at once, shocked and gratified at the candidness with which Anne's father discussed his background. Though such a disclosure seemed surprising, Nathan felt that he was a viable member of the family to be hearing all of this.

As he told it, Lieutenant Wood was born in 1734, the youngest son of James Wood. Like all of his older brothers, the lieutenant's given name, Josiah, began with the letter *J*, as did his own father's name. James

Wood was raised by a family of Quakers living in the Lehigh Valley of Pennsylvania who found him as a baby wrapped in deerskins and lying on their doorstep in the autumn of 1692. Lieutenant Wood noted that his father would be celebrating his ninety-ninth birthday, if he were still alive.

Lieutenant Wood added that while the adoptive family whose name was Austin was not willing to give the foundling their surname, they nevertheless called the boy James. When young James was to be registered at the Quaker school, Mr. Austin gave the boy a contrived family name of Wood, which was in reference to the place from which he came.

Nathan was stunned. Though careful not to disclose his thoughts, it occurred to him that the lieutenant was indeed the very grandson (and his wife, Anne, was the great-granddaughter) of the old woman with whom he made a secret pact … the old woman who lived atop the mountain that overlooked the very homes of her descendants.

Chapter 33

There was no way that Nathan was going to inform the lieutenant about Lydia Thorn; not at this point to be sure. After Lieutenant Wood finished his story, Nathan diverted the gentleman by asking him how he met George Washington. When Anne's father finished that story, which was long and drawn out, Nathan said that it was time to return to Greenfield.

During the trip home, Nathan asked, "Have you ever heard about your grandfather before?"

"Oh yes, on several occasions. We just don't talk about it to others much."

"Why didn't you tell me?"

"You never asked. What does it matter anyway?" she said. "My father fought in the war against the French and then fought again against the English. He raised his family on land that was ceded to him for his bravery in battle. He's a hero. What does it matter where his father came from?"

Nathan thought about this for a while as his horse pulled their chaise up-river. He did not answer right away. "You're right, what difference would it make?" For the time, Nathan felt it best to leave well enough alone.

During the next several weeks, as the earth warmed with the northern progression of the sun, the discovery gnawed at Nathan. He kept it to himself and, in doing so, aroused the suspicions of his wife that he was hiding something. Her oft-repeated requests for him to come out with it fell on deaf ears. He pretended not to know what she was talking about.

She even tried to use her favors as bargaining chips. He repeatedly shrugged her off by saying she was just addled with her pregnancy. As her abdomen swelled, she indeed looked the part of an expectant mother. Even her parents commented during their Sunday visits on how much she was beginning to show.

The longer he kept silent about what he knew, the more difficult it became for Nathan to approach the subject with Anne. He feared that such a startling revelation might well prove to be harmful to the baby. On more than one occasion, he set off towards Devil's Knob. Such courage was short lived, however, in spite of the fact that the actual truth was burning within him.

He decided that he would tell Anne about her great-grandmother after the baby was born. Then, they could decide together on what to do about telling Anne's father. As the days grew longer and hotter, Nathan kept his counsel. It was now summer. Time and circumstance would take care of themselves.

Chapter 34

The summer of 1791 was as terribly hot as the winter preceding it was brutally cold. Such seasonal extremes, though not peculiar to Virginia, were certainly not characteristic either. In the lowlands of Tidewater, yellow fever ravished slave and master alike. The higher elevations, with their inherent climatic and demographic advantages, were less prone to such depopulating epidemics. Yet, the usual problems of heat and humidity were nevertheless present in Nelson County on that particular summer.

As July boiled into August, Anne sweltered under the weight of her growing abdomen. The life that lived within was sapping her energy that was already waning from the oppressive effects of summer. Being indoors only served to protect her from the burning sun but did nothing to assuage the onslaught of heat and humidity.

All-too-brief respites came in the form of breezes, which invariably preceded torrential thunderstorms from the south. Aside from these occasional winds, her only relief was to sit on the banks of the Rockfish River and allow her bare feet to dangle in its cooling waters.

Often, she sat with her husband as he fished for trout that ran plentifully in the wake of its stream. They shared a golden apple and spent time just speculating on the gender of their unborn baby.

It was on one of these afternoons in mid-August that the expectant couple was discussing an upcoming visit by Anne's parents when a stray black cat approached. They had never before seen the feline and it purred as it brushed against Anne's back.

"It seems as though you've made a new friend," Nathan commented.

"I wonder where she might have come from." Anne stroked the animal's furry back. She offered a bit of apple to it, which it accepted and sampled with the discerning taste of a most particular bent.

"I don't much care for cats," Nathan intoned.

"Oh hush … don't be offensive to our guest." She laughed. "That's a good kitty." She stroked its back again. "I think I'll call you Midnight."

"Why Midnight?"

"Why not?"

"It's the middle of the afternoon," he teased, "for one thing."

"Her name is Midnight." Anne raised her beautiful chin in mock defiance. "Because she's so black, that's what I'm going to call her."

"I don't care what you call her as long as Midnight keeps the mice away and stays out of the house."

"Humph," Anne jerked her head.

Nathan looked at the cat and gently placed his right hand under its chin. "Do you understand, Midnight?" Nathan asked the cat. He feigned a frown.

Little did Nathan or Anne realize that the cat completely understood *everything* they said.

Chapter 35

The inferno that was August on Greenfield Farm did not let up until the second week of September. The lengthening shadows seemed to moderate temperatures, and this was more than welcomed by the woman who was in the midst of her eighth month. Since June, the Sunday visits with Anne's parents took place at Greenfield. Anne's mother insisted that her daughter refrain from traveling.

Midnight, the cat, remained close to the house. She spent much of her time on the open porch and was careful not to enter. Before the heat subsided, she found refuge beneath the porch or under the stairs leading up to it. She seemed to enjoy the gentle breezes that blew across its floorboards.

Frequently, the cat sat on the windowsill and stared into the house. When Anne caught the cat doing this at night, she opened the window as an invitation to allow Midnight to enter. Invariably, however, the feline leaped off the sill and onto the porch, refusing to enter.

"That cat seems to understand English," Nathan said. "I told it to stay out of the house and it obeys. I haven't seen many mice lately either. Maybe I'll let it stay around for a while longer." He enjoyed teasing Anne this way who became quite attached to her pet.

In spite of that summer's extreme weather, Nathan looked forward to a bounteous harvest. The corn crop was fair, and the squash and beans looked promising. He felt there was enough to eat that winter and this was always on his mind when he looked at the rows that he cultivated. Working the land was a struggle to survive and he never lost sight of that fact.

He still thought about the old woman. He wondered how he was going to introduce her to her great granddaughter. He prayed she would be there to help his wife give birth. Her attending to Anne's labor would conveniently enable him to unload the burdensome secret that he carried around with him since the previous March. Given the exciting prospect of a new baby and the opportunity of easing his own conscience, he could not wait until October brought Lydia Thorn to his doorstep.

Chapter 36

October brought the colors of fire to the Blue Ridge as well as to the lands that lay beneath. On clear days when there was no haze, the brilliant autumn sun electrified its rich colors. The trees seemed to radiate their own light from within. Brightly speckled hues, which painted the millions of broadleaf trees that covered the land, were only momentarily broken where man forged his clearings. From high atop the ridge, one could imagine the valley resembling a patch-worked quilt of amber squares that were the farms which lay amongst the vast and colored forest. On one of these farms, a man and a woman were awaiting the birth of their firstborn child.

Nathan long since harvested the fine crop of beans that would sustain his fledgling family. In early October, he began to gather the ears of corn. He saw better corn crops in his twenty-five years, but this year's harvest would not be the worst he had ever seen, either.

After collecting the edible corn, the stalks needed to be gathered and tied. Having done so, the next task was to cut the pumpkins and squash from their creeping vines and gather them before the frosts set in. Such was the season to reap what had earlier been sown ... to profit from what was invested. In his fields, Nathan worked and waited ...

In the warmth of summer, Lydia found relief from the congestive cough that plagued her that previous winter. At times, she dragged her rocking chair onto the porch and inhaled the warm breezes that proved to be therapeutic to her system. In doing so, she regained some of her strength and was faring quite well by the time the leaves began to change color.

In the month prior to the autumnal equinox, a deep sense of impending doom took hold of Lydia's psyche in a way she had not felt since her sad days in Maryland. Tituba was nearby and she could *feel* it in her veins. After all these decades, she had been found. Lydia's blood ran cold in spite of the warm air.

Now lacking the desire to flee as she might have fled in decades past, Lydia would have to take on Tituba for one final struggle. A struggle that would, most likely, mean the end of them both. She hoped she could deliver Nathan's child before this final conflict. She felt a deep obligation to the young man in whom she placed so much trust.

In the third week of October, Lydia sensed that the time had come for her to descend the mountain for one last trip. As she had so often done in the past, Lydia went to the corner of her room, picked up her broom and carried it to the porch. Placing it behind her, she closed her eyes and was aloft.

Chapter 37

Anne's labor began shortly after noon. She finished preparing the midday meal and started toward the front porch to summon her husband when she felt a sharp pain. Without having experienced such a pain before, she nevertheless knew what it meant. The baby was coming. She sat in a chair, doubled over in agony and held her stomach with both of her arms.

After a few terrible minutes, the pain subsided. She pulled herself up and opened the door. Walking onto the porch, Anne banged the saucepan with a wooden spoon. Nathan, who was only a few hundred yards away, sat a pumpkin into the cart and walked toward the house.

As he neared, he saw that she did not look well. He quickened his pace.

"Are you okay?" he inquired.

"It's time," she replied grabbing her stomach.

"Oh honey, oh my ..." Nathan's eyes widened. "You best lay down."

He took hold of her left arm and walked her toward their bed. Supporting the nape of her neck with his right hand he eased her backwards.

"Dinner's on the table," she said weakly.

"I don't want to eat." He nervously laughed at such a suggestion.

Fifteen minutes passed and Anne was experiencing her second labor pain.

"Oh … NATHAN!" she yelled.

Her voice was uncharacteristically deep and harsh. He grabbed her hand but felt helpless. Shocked at the strength with which she squeezed his left hand, he had not imagined such a grip could be had from such delicate hands as hers.

Outside there arose a commotion. Midnight was fighting with another cat and the screeching was quite terrible and sufficiently loud enough to permeate the interior of the house.

"What's going on?" Anne asked.

"Midnight's having it out with another stray," he answered. "When I was gathering pumpkins, I saw this light gray cat prowling around. I thought it was Midnight and that she'd gotten herself dusty. But then, I noticed that the gray cat had the most beautiful blue eyes. It wasn't Midnight."

"Do something," she protested. "They'll kill each other."

"There's no way I'm going to leave you … surely not for two cats fighting."

"But Midnight?" she offered.

"Look Anne … Midnight probably feels like she is protecting you. She's going to be fine … and I'm not going to get in the middle of it."

Nathan was trying to comfort his wife. There was no way he could have assumed which of the two cats would prevail. He didn't care much either for he never did learn to like cats. Since his wife was so deeply attached to her black cat, he silently hoped that Midnight would prove his theory and emerge victorious.

Lydia knew at once that the black cat sitting on the porch of Nathan's house was her lifelong nemesis, Tituba. Before she could be seen by Nathan, she assumed the form of a cat. To mortal ears, only the screeching of two felines in battle could be heard. But the two cats were fiercely arguing with one another, as they began their fight.

"There's a baby about to be born and I'm going to kill it," Tituba said. "And there's nothing you can do to stop me."

"Haven't you killed enough?" Lydia asked. "You caused the death of all those innocent people in Salem with your wicked stories, and you killed Little Sean McComas, you wretched bitch!"

"McComas wasn't the only life I took. Several children turned up missing in Baltimore over the years, and everyone thought that it was *Lydia Thistle* who had done it. Your name is reviled up and down the Chesapeake, girl." Tituba laughed.

"You won't kill anyone else." Lydia screeched. "Not unless you kill me first."

Lydia lunged at Tituba. The two wrestled in the front yard of Nathan Greens' house. Tituba took a swipe at Lydia's face and her claws slashed Lydia's right cheek. Lydia fell back. Tituba pounced and bit Lydia's neck. Lydia used her hind legs to kick at Tituba's underbelly. Tituba screeched in pain as the two somersaulted ever closer toward the edge of the Rockfish River.

Tituba sunk her teeth into Lydia's neck just barely missing her main artery. Lydia, by using her hind legs, managed to tear into the abdomen of her adversary, doing much damage to the walls of Tituba's stomach. As they were just at the edge of the river, Lydia sprang Tituba into the air with a sudden force from her hind legs.

Craftily landing on her feet, Tituba growled with delight at having backed Lydia against the river's edge. With a sudden lurch, she sprang at Lydia. Lydia rolled sideways and Tituba leapt unwittingly headfirst into the deep water. She wailed just before hitting the surface. She screamed once more before disappearing beneath the steady flow. Tituba had, at long last, gone to the devil and could bother Lydia no more.

Chapter 38

Inside the house, Anne was in the midst of her third contraction. The screeching outside was growing more vicious but its importance was superseded by labor pains. As the third wave subsided, the screeching seemed to be moving away toward the river.

When Anne was able to, she asked about Midnight. Her husband said that the two cats were wrestling and rolling toward the river's edge, but he encouragingly reported that Midnight seemed to be prevailing in the struggle. As he watched through the window, Nathan could only see that the black cat was on top of the gray one and presumably would win.

Before the fight ended, Anne was in the throes of yet another contraction, which seemed to occur sooner than what had been the case before. Neither of them witnessed the grizzly conclusion to the feline struggle. The screeching stopped with Anne's fourth contraction.

Two more contractions came ten minutes apart, followed by a sudden knock at the door.

Lydia lay alongside the river still in the form of a gray cat. After a few minutes, she struggled and rose to her feet. Slowly, she made her way up the hill to the place where she originally changed form. No matter what, she was determined to die as a human. Her face, neck and sides were bleeding from the painful scratches that covered her body. Having reassumed human form, she grimaced at the feel of the woolen clothing on her cuts. She managed to pick up her broom and winced again as she held it under her seat.

She might have walked the couple of hundred yards, but her legs were sore. She chose to fly. She landed on the top of the stairs and feeling dazed, nearly tumbled to what might have been a certain death. With the broom's worn handle, she rapped at the oaken door.

"Who could that be?" Anne asked.

"I bet I know." Nathan walked to the door.

He found Lydia scratched and bleeding about her face and neck. Anne was stunned at the appearance of the old woman who looked as though she had been worked over with a cat-o'-nine-tails.

"What happened, Lydia?" Nathan grabbed the woman by her right arm. "You look dreadful."

"Water, get me some water." Lydia gasped.

Nathan brought her a bucket of water and some rags. He handed her the ladle. She took a good swallow and returned the ladle to Nathan. He handed her a rag that he had soaked, and with it she wiped the scratches and cuts on her face and neck.

Anne went into another contraction before the two could be formally introduced. In spite of her own condition, Lydia summoned the instinctive force that sustained her and went to the woman who was about to give birth.

"How long has it been since your last pain?" Lydia asked the young woman.

"Just before you knocked on the door," Nathan answered.

"It's coming soon. Nathan, get me some hot water, scissors and twine. We don't have much time."

Fortunately, Anne had not changed out of the nightgown she had worn the night before. It was a simple matter for the elderly midwife to raise the patient's gown and go to work. When Anne felt another contraction, this one more severe than any she had thus far encountered, Lydia told Nathan to bring her broom over to the bed.

"Now bite down on this and push," the old woman said gently placing the broom's handle in Anne's mouth. Anne did exactly as she was told. There was something about this scratched-up old woman that seemed safe and reassuring. With each subsequent contraction, Anne was instructed to bite down on the broom handle and push. With a final thrust, her baby was born.

"Nathan, you've got yourself a baby girl," the old lady said looking over at the father. As instructed, he handed Lydia the scissors. Having bound the umbilical stump, she handed the baby to Nathan.

"Anne, we've got a little girl …" He cried. "We've got a little baby girl."

The baby cried the moment it was born and was still crying when her father received her from the midwife. Though exhausted, Lydia tended to the afterbirth, which she placed into an empty chamber pot at the foot of the bed.

Anne was doing well, all things considered. As Nathan took the baby to her mother, Lydia said that the little girl might be hungry.

"Let me show you what to do," Lydia offered. She placed the baby to Anne's left breast and the baby took to it with much enthusiasm. "That's a mighty pretty daughter you have there."

Nathan smiled and stood tall. "This is going to take some explaining," he said. "Lydia you … you just brought your own great-great granddaughter into the world."

"What?" the women said in unison.

Nathan pieced together the entire story as he knew it. The women listened intently while the baby, who was still unnamed, fed at her mother's breast. When he finished his story, Anne and Lydia were both crying.

Wiping her eyes, Lydia took a deep breath and shook her head. After substantiating the essence of what Nathan had said, there was no doubt as to the bloodline that ran between the three generations of females that fate conspired to unite in a room on that October afternoon.

"I always did like haggling with your father," Lydia said to Anne. "If I knew he was my grandson, I might have received a better trade."

They all laughed.

"This is the secret I wanted to tell you, Anne," he said. "I believe your father needs to meet his grandmother."

"Father will be here day after tomorrow," Anne said. "What a wonderful day that will be."

"If I am going to meet my grandson, I'd best be getting myself cleaned up. I'll go back to my house and get ready." Lydia smiled. Her smile belied the *intense* pain she was experiencing.

"You never did say what happened to your face," Nathan frowned and waited for an answer.

"Your cat took a disliking to me and scratched me up right good," she said.

There was no need to divulge to the two mortals information relating to the ability of witches to change their physical form.

"Was it a black cat or a gray cat?" Nathan was pressing the point.

"A black cat," Lydia replied.

"I'm sorry," Anne said. "Midnight got into a bad fight with a stray earlier. It must have made her frightened of strangers."

"No matter," Lydia answered. "I'll be leaving now."

"Can't you stay?" Nathan asked.

"Nonsense, boy," she scolded. "I've got to get ready." With that, she picked up her broom, and a gust of wind blew open the door.

"Take my horse," Nathan offered.

"What do I need with a horse?" Lydia laughed. She sat on her broom and was gone. The door slammed shut behind her.

"Well, I'll ..." Anne started to say.

Nathan interrupted her. "I know what you mean. Believe me, I know *just* what you mean."

Nathan turned his attention toward his daughter who, by now, was asleep. "What do you think we should call her?"

"I know what I'd like to call her," Anne yawned. "Naming her is supposed to be yours to do, husband."

"Are you thinking what I'm thinking?" he asked, almost playfully.

"If you're thinking *Lydia?*" Anne yawned, again.

"Lydia Green ..." He smiled, "... today is your birthday."

She closed her eyes and before long, Anne, too, was sound asleep.

Chapter 39

Nathan and Anne looked upon their baby with a deep sense of joy and wonderment that they not felt before. Baby Lydia was healthy and beautiful, and her parents were surprised to find that when she opened her sapphire-blue eyes, they resembled those of her great-great grandmother.

For her own part, the infant cooed and cawed the very next morning. This intensified her parents' curiosity to an even greater degree. Their first day as parents passed largely without incident. Nathan remembered the cart of pumpkins he left in the middle of the field. He excused himself to finish the task but only managed to stay away from his fledgling family for less than an hour. He missed them that much.

The next morning, Anne's parents arrived and were quite surprised to learn that the baby was here. Mrs. Wood rocked and lavished attention on the baby. Anne took her father out on the porch for a private conversation. She explained her discovery of his grandmother as best she could, and he listened intently to what she had to say.

Lieutenant Wood was startled upon hearing that the old woman, with whom he had done business for so many years, was his own grandmother. He confessed that he always enjoyed their haggling and that he found her bargaining skills to be a source of amazement, but he never imagined that this was the mother of his very own father.

Anne informed her father that his grandmother would be paying a visit on that afternoon. He replied that he would like a moment to discuss the matter with Mrs. Wood, so Anne called Nathan out onto the porch. The lieutenant went into the house and told his wife all about what Anne had to say.

While the baby's grandparents conferred, the new parents stood on the porch and looked out toward the river. Nathan put his arm around his wife and thanked her for giving him the family that he had always wanted, but never thought that he would have. Anne said nothing and leaned her head against her husband's chest.

As the hours passed, there was no sign of Lydia. The dead silence that filled the room with anticipation only exacerbated the tension of awaiting a guest who would not arrive. When the sun set behind Devil's Knob, they all agreed that something prevented Lydia from making the journey to Greenfield as she promised. The Woods decided to stay the night. It would enable the men to get an early start. They would ascend the mountain to see if Lydia was all right. As the baby fed at her mother's breast, Mrs. Wood prepared the evening meal.

While Nathan, his wife and mother-in-law ate heartily, Lieutenant Wood only picked at his plate. The revelation of his own grandmother was too much for him. Later on, his sleep proved to be just as elusive.

Chapter 40

Nathan Green set out the next morning along with his father-in-law. The climb up Devil's Knob was as slow as it was steep. As they did not want to risk their horses on such a treacherous journey, they set out on foot. Because of the lieutenant's age, Nathan took his time stopping periodically to allow his wife's father to catch his breath.

The morning was crisp and cool. The sky was unblemished save for a bank of clouds on the eastern horizon. The trees, having passed their fiery peaks of color, were mostly brown. As the two climbers attained higher elevation, leaves that had clung to the trees now littered the ground on which they tread. By the time they neared the top of the mountain, most of the limbs were barren.

Nathan and the lieutenant noticed as they approached the cabin that it seemed to be unoccupied. Nathan called out to Lydia but there was no answer. He told his father-in-law that they should go inside but the older man demurred. The two sat on Lydia's porch and looked out upon the valley.

Nathan then felt it necessary to tell the lieutenant of the solemn promise he had made to Lydia. Lieutenant Wood, in finding out that his grandmother was a witch and therefore faced eternal damnation unless her wishes were carried out, agreed to go into the house with his son-in-law. As they entered the single room, they saw that they were alone.

Precisely as she had foretold, Nathan found a pile of ashes in front of the fire. "These are the remains of your grandmother."

The lieutenant sat in the rocking chair and wept. "There is only one thing to do Nathan."

In the corner of the room they spotted a cauldron. As the two men gathered up the ashes, they carefully placed them inside. When they could scoop no more, Nathan grabbed the ancient broom.

Tied to its worn handle, was a tag:

Give this to the baby when she is old enough to understand.

Without removing the tag, Nathan swept up the remaining ashes into a pile that the lieutenant painstakingly placed into the cauldron. He showed the lieutenant the tag and the older man acknowledged it with a single nod. Nathan carried the cauldron of ashes, and his father-in-law held onto the broom of Lydia Thorn.

On the afternoon of October 24, 1791, two men climbed to the summit of Devil's Knob. One carried a broom and the other carried a cauldron of ashes. When they reached the top, they looked around. Toward the east, they saw the tiny rooftops that were their homes. To the west, they beheld a lush and promising valley that beckoned future settlements. As a gust of wind blew up the shady eastern slope of Devil's Knob, Nathan Green cast the remains of Lydia Thorn into the breeze that carried her to her deliverance.

On her sixteenth birthday in 1807, Lydia Green was presented with a most unusual gift. An ancient broom that belonged to her great-great grandmother. It bore a faded tag with handwriting that was barely legible. Along with the broom, she heard a story that she passed down to her own children.

It was the story of a determined young woman who, in spite of personal disaster and tragedy, was ever-present to help life renew itself. Through the generations that would be caught in times of war and peace, depression and prosperity, and tragedy and triumph the story of a broom and the woman to whom it once belonged would be told and retold, again and again.

FINIS

CPSIA information can be obtained
at www.ICGtesting.com
Printed in the USA
JSHW041507071120
9399JS00001B/2